You Can't Fight Love 2

By

Nona Day

SOUL Publications

Crue

The phone call I'd just received caused me to swerve over into the next lane, nearly hitting a car. I was rushing through traffic trying to get to the hospital with Zelda all while losing my mind. I had t o figure out how I was going to get the money to save Quaysha's life. Loud horns honked snatching me away from my trance. Zelda and Quay were in their life-threatening situations because of me. I thought Khalil had left Atlanta, because I hadn't heard from him since Chike almost killed him. Khalil was plotting his revenge to get back the money I stole from him. Quay never wanted to rob him; I was the one that convinced her to come with me. Plus, I brought my secrets into Zelda's home and now she was fighting for her life. Everything around me was a blur as I sped through traffic, but I made sure to stay as close to the ambulance as I could.

Once we arrived at the hospital, they rushed Zelda inside. There was no valet at the emergency room entrance, so I had to park my car. After I made it inside, I went straight to the desk to get information on Zelda. I bombarded the receptionist with question after question, but she had no information for me. All I could do was pace the floor and wait for someone to come tell me something.

While waiting on news about Zelda, I prayed hard for her to pull through. As soon as my prayer ended, I thought of Quaysha. I knew she was scared out of her mind, because my mind was on overload and I wasn't the one who was kidnapped. There was no doubt in my mind, Khalil would kill her if I didn't pay him. Feeling helpless, I flopped down on a chair. Remembering I needed to call Jedrek, I dialed his number again. Once again, he sent me straight to voicemail.

It felt like hours were passing by, but no one had come to tell me anything. I walked back up to the nurse's station; I could tell the receptionist was getting agitated with me, but I didn't give a damn. When she saw me approaching the window, she rolled her eyes and turned her head.

"You can take that rude ass look off your face and tell me something about my cousin. All you've done since I've been here is talk on your damn cellphone. I'm sure that's against company policy," I stated, belligerently.

"And I'm going to tell you like I've told you the other four times, the doctor will come let you know something when he's able," she said bopping her head.

"I've been here for hours. What are they doing?" I asked angrily.

An older white nurse approached the window. "Ma'am, I know you are worried about your cousin. I promise you they are doing everything they can to save her. It hasn't been hours since they brought her in; she's only been here for fifty-three minutes," she let me know.

Time was moving so slow. It felt like I had been there for hours. The black nurse smirked at me, and I wanted to reach behind the counter and pull that cheap ass wig off her head.

"Well, you need to teach this unprofessional bitch some respect and compassion," I said referring to the black nurse. When I turned to walk back to my seat, my cellphone rang. I closed my eyes not wanting to answer this call, but I had to. I knew Vanity was calling, because she hadn't heard from Zelda. I cleared my throat before answering.

"Hi Van," I said with a trembling voice.

"What's wrong, Crue? Where's Zelda?" she asked.

She was trying to remain calm, but I could hear the fear and stress in her voice. My actions weren't only affecting Zelda and Quaysha, they were going to affect everyone that loved and cared for them. When that realization set in, I couldn't hold it in any longer. All I could do was break down and cry.

"Crue, where are you?" Vanity asked, nervously. I couldn't stop crying long enough to tell her what had happened. Someone snatched my phone from me, but I was too distraught to argue with whoever took it. I fell back in the seat and let my emotions out.

"It's me. I found her at Emory," Echon informed Vanity. I stopped crying, relieved to have someone here with me. I knew Vanity had gone into panic mode, because Echon was trying to calm her down. He told her to stay home with the babies, but she wasn't having it.

"Stay there until Chike comes to get you. Vanity don't come here alone. Stay there," he demanded before he hung up and called Chike.

He walked away with my phone with Chike on the other end. Reality hit me once again. Now, I had to tell him about what happened to Quaysha. If he doesn't kill me, Jedrek will. *When I get the information that Zelda is going to be okay. I will put all my effort into getting Quaysha back safely.* I promised myself. I just didn't need them knowing I was the cause of all of this. At least not until I had fixed everything.

After ending his call, Echon came and sat beside me. He wasn't a man of many words, so we sat quietly until I broke the silence.

"I called Jedrek, but the call dropped when I told him what happened. I don't know if he heard what I said," I informed him.

"He heard you. He'll be here," he said glancing at me. Something in his eyes gave me an eerie feeling; I didn't know if Jedrek coming home was a good or bad thing. We sat quietly until a tall, sun-tanned white woman approached us.

"Are you here for Ms. Vandross?" she asked, glancing at us. We stood up at the same time.

"Yea," Echon answered. I held my breath praying for the best.

"I'm Dr. Kelton. May I ask your relation to her?" she asked. I wasn't in the state of mind to deal with the bureaucratic shit you go through about next of kin.

"What da fuck does it matter? Just tell us how she's doing," I demanded. Echon quickly gave me a look that sent chills through me, and I calmed down instantly.

"I'm sorry. It's hospital policy. We have to know the relationship to the patient before we can share any information," she explained.

"I understand. I'm her brother-in-law. This is her niece. Please excuse her behavior; she's just concerned and scared," Echon said politely. This was the most I'd ever heard him talk. I always thought he was a little slow, but I guess not.

"I understand. Ms. Vandross was shot in the lower left chest area. I'm sorry to say…," she said before I let out a heart-breaking cry. I knew nothing good was going to come behind the last four words she spoke. I felt Dr. Kelton put her arm around me to calm me down.

"She's still here," she said calmly. I cried harder apologizing for what I caused, and relieved to know I hadn't lost my cousin. I looked up at Echon and he was just staring at me emotionless.

"What are you sorry about?" Echon asked. I was glad Dr. Kelton spoke, to avoid me having to answer his question.

"Her condition is very serious. We have her stable for now, but we need to go in and remove the bullet. It's very close to her heart. We need the next of kin to sign the forms."

"Her parents stay in Las Vegas," I told her.

"How soon does the surgery need to be done?" Echon asked.

"As soon as possible," she informed us.

"Can her sister sign?" Echon asked.

"Yes, absolutely," she said eagerly.

I looked up to see Vanity, the babies and Chike approaching us. Chike had Lil J in his arms while Vanity held her daughter, Blessing. That wasn't her name but that was what we called her. They gave her an African name in honor of Echon's parents. After Echon introduced Vanity to Dr. Kelton, she gave me Blessing, and they walked over to talk in private. I kept my eyes focused on Blessing, because if I looked into Chike's mean eyes, he would have known I had something to do with this. He sat across from me. I didn't have to look up to feel his eyes burning a hole through me. Maybe it was paranoia, but it was like his eyes pierced my soul.

Hours Before

Jedrek

I thought giving birth to my son was the scariest thing I'd ever had to face. I realized that wasn't fear. That was nerves, excitement and joy. Sitting here waiting for Drekia to risk her life to have a normal life was fear. The thought of this possibly being the last time I would get to talk to her was causing me to second guess her choice to have the surgery. I was still her guardian and could end this all before it happened. The thought of doing just that was deep in my mind.

We sat in Drekia's hospital room listening to Dr. Abei go over the procedure for the third time today. I glanced at Drekia to see if she was sure about her decision. Her body was poised, and her face was relaxed. She didn't seem to have an ounce of worry or fear in her. Vonna sat on the opposite side of Drekia's bed texting on her phone. The only reason she was here was because Drekia wanted her here. I hadn't forgotten that she had Drekia thinking I wanted to send her to a mental institution.

"Does everyone understand how this procedure will work? Any questions?" Dr. Abei asked glancing at us as he stood at the foot of the bed. Drekia nodded her head with a smile. Vonna looked up and smiled at him. I understood what would happen during the procedure. I just wasn't as confident as Drekia was about having it. My gut feeling was telling me to cancel this surgery. I excused myself and walked out into the hallway. I dialed Zelda's phone number.

"Hi," she answered quickly.

"How y'all doing?" I asked.

"We're doing fine. He's a greedy boy like his daddy. Vanity is picking him up in a few. She wants her quality time with him While he's with them, I'm going to get some work done I promise I won't overdo it" she said.

I couldn't see her smiling, but I knew she was. Her smile, body, and soul gave me life. You could only fight a feeling for so long before it finally took control of you. I was in love with her, I just hadn't spoken the words to her. But I couldn't deny it anymore. There was a moment of dead silence before she spoke.

"I know this has to be scary for you. This is what is called unconditional love. You are willing to risk breaking your heart to give Drekia what she wants. You raised a fearless, strong, young woman through all your struggles and her condition," she said.

"Thank you," I said graciously. I didn't know why I called her, but I felt like I needed to hear her say something. She said what I needed to hear.

She giggled. "I would pray with you over the phone, but I'm just learning all about praying. When we hang up, call Vanity and tell her to pray with you."

"I know we can't have sex, and I can't eat you for six weeks, but you gon' give me some of that fire head when I get home?" I asked. It sounded like a joke, but I was dead serious. Six weeks with none of her was too much.

She laughed. "Bye Jedrek."

"Yo, hold up before you hang up the phone," I said quickly.

"What?" she asked still laughing. Another dead silence traveled between us. I cleared my throat and said it.

"I love you." I never gave her a chance to reply before ending the call.

I had never feared love, there just wasn't a place in my life to love a woman like Zelda. When love hits you, you'd find a way to make a place for that person regardless of your situation. I took her advice and called Vanity. After telling her to check in on Zelda and Lil J, I asked her to pray with me. She happily fulfilled my request. I believed in God, but never had I needed Him more than now. I listened as Vanity prayed. I put all my faith in His hands to let His will be done. When we were done praying, I went back into the room.

"I'm ready," I said. Drekia gave me a big smile. She knew I was having second thoughts.

"Can I speak to my brother alone first?" Drekia asked Dr. Abei.

He nodded his head. "I'll be back in fifteen minutes."

"Mama give me a few minutes with Drek," Drekia said.

"What you got to say to him that I can't hear?" Vonna asked.

I gave her a look to let her know to leave the room, and she reluctantly left. Drekia reached her arm out for me to take her hand. I walked over, held her hand and sat down beside her bed. She gave me the warmest smile while gently holding my hand.

"I know you were having second thoughts but thank you for coming around. I know I've been hell to deal with this past year, and I'm sorry," she said.

"Drekia, you ain't gotta apologize to me for nothing. You my baby sister. It ain't shit in this world I wouldn't do for you," I assured her. She wiped the single tear that slid from her eye.

"That's why I love you so much. You never left my side. I know it hasn't been easy for you. You were just a kid yourself trying to raise a mentally challenged younger sister. You put your life on hold for me. I want you to promise me something," she said squeezing my hand.

"What?" I asked.

"Drek, if I don't come through this surgery, I don't want you to let guilt or regret consume your life. I don't remember everything that caused me to be in this condition, but I know you put the blame on yourself. Please don't do that again; release that guilt. You have a beautiful woman and handsome son who needs you. I want you to live the life you deserve. You've giving me so much happiness over the years. I want to know that you'll be as happy as you've made my life," she said.

"Is this why you doing this? You think I ain't happy with you in my life?" I asked angrily. My first thought was that this was some shit Vonna was putting in her head.

"No, so calm down. I'm doing this because I want to do it for myself. My life is great. It's not that I'm unappreciative of what God has given me, because I am. I also feel as if God has put this chance before me for a reason. Whatever His will is, will be," she said smiling.

"You ain't gon' die, Drekia," I said trying to convince myself more than her.

She winked at me and smiled. "I know."

About Three Hours Later

Dr. Abei said the surgery would take eight hours. It felt like time had stopped, and every ten minutes I was checking the time. Vonna sat next to me asking me a million questions about what could go wrong with the surgery. Her negativity was too much for me, so I left her sitting in the family waiting room and walked downstairs. I needed to get outside and get some fresh air. As I was checking the time again, Crue called my phone. My chest felt as if it was caving in. I knew something had to be wrong. After answering her call, the only thing I remembered her saying was Zelda got shot before my phone slipped from my hand.

I needed to get home as soon as possible. I called the airline to find the next flight to Atlanta. There wasn't a flight out until six o'clock in the morning, but I couldn't wait that long. I needed to get home to Zelda and our son. There was only one person I knew could get me a flight home now. I called Bull and he told me he would have a private plane ready for me in a couple of hours. My mind struggled with leaving Drekia on the operating table, but I knew she would understand. I went back into the waiting room to let Vonna know I'd be leaving. She quickly hung up her phone when she saw me walking toward her.

"I need you to be here for Drekia when she wakes up from surgery. Zelda has been shot, and I need to get home," I told her.

She jumped up from the chair. "Your sister is on that table fighting for her life, and you gon' leave her for a bitch?"

If she wasn't my mother, I would have slapped the shit out of her. Aunt Dee always raised me to respect Vonna regardless of her actions. She has never been a mother to Drekia or me, and sometimes, I forgot she was the woman that birthed me. I didn't feel the need to explain myself to her, so I just walked away. I could hear her cussing me out as I walked back toward the elevator.

I didn't waste time going back to the hotel to pack; I took a taxi to the airstrip to take my flight home. Before my flight, I called Echon, because Crue was a total mess on the phone, so I knew she was in no condition to answer any questions. Whoever was responsible for this would pay with their life. The ten-hour flight home felt like ten years. I passed the time by imagining the horrific death of whoever was responsible for shooting Zelda.

Chike

"Kill whoever you need to kill to find out what you need to know about this. Save the snake's head for Jedrek. He's on his way home," Echon instructed me. I nodded my head.

Jedrek was like an older brother to me. He took me off the corners working for pennies and gave me the opportunity to be able to provide a home for my daughter. I was a troubled teen and in and out of the system for years. It wasn't my mother's fault; she did the best she could as a single mom. The sperm donor was never a father to me, because I was an outside child that he never claimed.

Jedrek did more than take me off the streets, he educated me on making legit money by opening my own businesses. At twenty-five years old, I was doing damn good for myself and my daughter. My goal was to get in the position to leave the drug game behind me.

"How do you know Drek's on his way home?" Crue asked Echon, eavesdropping on our conversation. She was holding Lil J in her arms.

"Why da fuck you in our conversation?" I asked angrily. I hated being around her. Everything about her made me feel shit I didn't want to feel.

"Fuck you! I wasn't talking to you," she said angrily.

"He called me after you called him," Echon answered her.

She rolled her eyes at me and walked over to sit next to Vanity. After me and Echon discussed a few things, we walked over to Vanity, Crue and the babies. He took Blessing from Vanity's arms.

"I need to pick up Quay," Crue said.

"Yes, go ahead. Zelda's parents should be here in a few hours," Vanity told her. She placed Lil J in Vanity's arms before giving her a hug.

"I'm going back to Zelda's house to look around. Jedrek will be able to look at the security monitors when he gets here," I told Echon.

I planned on going to Zelda's house, but I needed to catch up with Crue before she left the hospital. I had been calling Quaysha all day and all my calls had been going to voicemail. Something in my gut didn't feel right, and I was sure Crue was that something. I caught up with Crue just as she was getting in her car. Grabbing her arm, I stopped her from getting inside the car. She snatched away from me and started screaming. Her hand slapped me across the face so hard I almost slapped the shit out of her.

"Calm the fuck down!" I barked at her.

She finally opened her eyes to see it was me. "Why da fuck is you following me? Keep your hands off me!"

"Where's Quay?" I asked staring at her. The simple question caused her to tense up.

"If she hasn't told you, I guess she doesn't want you to know," she said nervously. It was obvious she was hiding something.

"Don't fuckin' play with me, Crue. Yo cousin laying in there with a bullet in her chest. If you know something about this, you better speak da fuck up. Better to tell me now than have Drek found out," I warned her.

It wasn't a threat to scare her. It was the truth. Jedrek wasn't going to give a damn about her being Zelda's cousin. Whatever she had going on, I was sure it had something to do with the nigga from the abortion clinic and that Quay was involved with it.

She stared at me. "I don't know anything about this. If I knew who did this to Zee, I would say it. As far as Quay goes, she's with her other nigga. I was trying to spare your feelings by saying she's at work. Now, get out my face."

I chuckled. It was obvious she was lying. Quay was a cool girl, but she couldn't hurt my feelings by fucking another nigga. I knew she wanted more with me, but I wasn't the type to play with her heart. I told her straight up, I wasn't looking for a relationship or love. She was good with us just kicking it as fuck buddies. My thoughts travelled back to the first night we fucked at Quan's apartment.

Everything was going good until Crue decided to show her childish ass. She didn't like seeing Quay doing drugs, and I did commend her for trying to look out for her friend. Quan used drugs too, but I was done trying to convince him to leave the shit alone. You couldn't use your own product in the drug game. He wasted a lot of his money on drugs and bullshit. After he gave Quay the Percocet, Crue went off. He hauled her ass into the bedroom to calm her down when she came at me for not speaking on Quay taking the pill. At that time, I didn't know she did drugs. Still, I didn't feel like it was my place to speak on it.

"I'm 'bout to get up outta here. Let Quan know I'm out," I said standing up from the table where Quay and I were sitting.

"No, you don't have to leave. You know they always argue then make up. Stay and keep me company," she said standing up quickly.

"Nah, I'm out. I got some shit I need to check up on anyway. You need to be careful about popping pills and shit, Quay. That shit can lead you into a black hole," I warned her.

She smiled and walked closer to me. "I like that you are concerned about me. I like you a lot, Chike."

"Come on, Quay. We've had this conversation too many times. I don't want you to get caught in your feelings about me. I like you but not on that level," I said.

"I know. I'm only trying to get to a certain level with you. We ain't gotta take it any farther than that," she said, stroking my crotch. The pill had kicked in, and she was feeling the high it was giving her. She shocked me when she dropped to her knees. I had done some grimy shit in my life, but I'd never taken advantage of a female.

"Woah!" I said backing away. I grabbed her arm and helped her to her feet.

"Yeah, I'm high but I know what I'm doing," she said taking my hand and leading me to the spare bedroom.

Quay fucked me like a porn star. Her head game was the best I ever had, and she rode my dick like a pro. When she rode me with my dick deep inside her ass, I exploded inside the condom so hard it busted. After I came, she licked my dick clean and sucked me back to life. My dick went soft when she tried to lick between my ass cheeks. Some freaky shit just wasn't for me and that was one of them.

Ever since that night, we'd been kicking it as fuck buddies and friends. I knew she was developing feelings for me. But she was just a distraction from the feelings I was starting to feel for Crue. I felt guilty as shit for fucking with her and using her to set my boundaries with her best friend. One of the reasons I was calling her today was to break things off with her, because she didn't deserve to be treated that way

There was also a side to Quay that made me want to be there for her. I watched Special, Krysta's mom, get hooked on drugs. Quay was only a casual user but that was the same way Special started. I overlooked warning signs of Special's addiction because I was in the streets making money. Maybe I could help Quay before she got to that point.

"Call Quay and tell her you on the way to pick her up," I said with a smirk. Before she could open her mouth to cuss me out, my phone rang. I immediately answered when I saw Ma's phone number.

"I'm sorry, Ma. I'm on the way," I said answering the call.

"I'm just calling to let you know I'm not going in to work tonight, so I got her," she said sounding tired.

"You okay?" I asked.

"Yeah, just got a headache," she said.

"I'll come get her, so you can get some rest," I told her.

"Boy, she's asleep. No point in waking her up. Just come get her tomorrow before I go to work. I'm going in at three o'clock, so be here about two," she told me.

"Thanks Ma," I said.

I still was going by to check on her, because it wasn't like Ma to miss work. She really had to be feeling bad to call in. Crue had gotten in her car and started it. I would have to get the truth from her later. I needed to check on Ma and Krysta first.

"Tell Quay to call me," I told Crue. She didn't reply to my comment before pulling off.

A Day Later

Quay

"This wasn't a part of the deal. Why are you doing this?" I asked as I sat in the hotel room with Khalil and his cousin, Mikah. I knew my life was in jeopardy. Khalil was going to kill me if Crue didn't come up with the money. Things weren't supposed to go this way. Khalil was never supposed seriously consider killing me. It was an only a threat to get the money from Crue. I guess now I would find out how much she valued our friendship.

"Well, some nigga was there picking her up at the clinic when I showed up. So, my plan didn't go through like I wanted," he said.

"That was my boyfriend you idiot! I sent him there to pick her up. You was supposed to get her at the house. How did you even know she was at the abortion clinic?" I asked him.

"She fucking a nigga name Gerard that I supply. We call him G. His shawty came to his spot raising hell 'bout Crue being pregnant for him. She told him you told her Crue was getting an abortion. That bitch acted a fool when

he said he was going to stop Crue from killing his seed,"
Mikah said laughing.

"Damn you a grimy ass friend. First, you get in touch
with me to set yo friend up. Then you rat her out to her
enemy," Khalil said laughing. I mistakenly told Lai about
the abortion. We were drinking and getting high one night
and it slipped out.

I rolled my eyes at him but didn't reply. He was right. I
was grimy. What I was doing was wrong, but so was Crue.
She was all about herself; she was only my best friend
when it suited her. Every time her life was going well, she
forgot all about me. When we were in high school, we were
inseparable until she got a nigga. Then, it was fuck Quay.
She came back around when I got new friends; she couldn't
stand seeing me have a life without her.

I'd always been like a charity case to her, and she
needed me to make her feel special. The sad part was I
needed her to make myself feel good. She thought I was
setup the night of the video of me in high school, but that
wasn't the case. I knew exactly what I was doing. I told
those girls to record me fucking that boy, because I wanted
boys to like me like they liked Crue, and all the popular
girls in school. The video backfired on me and humiliated

me. Instead of guys wanting to get with me, they bullied me. I played the victim role, because I knew Crue would defend me like she always did.

When we moved to Atlanta, things were no different. She got a boyfriend and forgot about me. When I became friends with Lai, she came back around again. I understood how our friendship worked, and I learned to accept that.

The final line had been drawn when I walked into Chike's mom's kitchen; I saw the way Crue glanced at Chike, and I felt the tension in the room between them. There was no doubt in my mind, she wanted Chike because she realized he was a better man than Quan, but there was no way I was going to let her have him. Ever since that night, Chike had been distant from me.

I sent him to the abortion clinic to pick her up, so he could see how trifling she was, hoping he would see she wasn't someone he wanted to be with, but Khalil fucked up the entire plan. It was time for me to experience what it felt like to be loved. Crue had always had niggas feeling her. I just wanted my chance.

"I can't believe you shot Zelda," I said feeling emotional.

I never meant for this to happen to Zelda. I told Khalil about all the expensive jewelry Zelda had at her house, and I gave them the security code to rob the house. I didn't know Zelda would be there.

"The bitch saw our face," Mikah said.

"Is she…?" I asked unable to say the word.

"Don't know and don't care. You better worry about your own life. If Crue doesn't come up with the hundred-grand, y'all both dead," he warned me.

"You promised me I would get thirty thousand of it," I reminded him.

"You get twenty thousand now," he said smiling at me.

"Jedrek is going to kill everyone responsible for shooting Zelda. You think you crazy, you don't know crazy," I warned him. They laughed.

"That nigga bleed just like us," Khalil said with a scowl on his face.

He didn't understand Jedrek has an army that would go to war for him. All he had was Mikah. With those odds, they would surely end up dead. My goal was to make sure I came out winning. The worst part of this entire setup was I couldn't talk to Chike. He had called my phone several times in the last twenty-four hours, but for this plan to work, I had to play my part. After making the call to Crue, Khalil destroyed my phone. He didn't want to take the chance of it being tracked.

We had moved to a different hotel. This was going to be the longest week of my life. I was ready to get back to Chike and start our life together. Mikah, Khalil's friend had gone out to get some food, so I decided to start the next part of my plan. Since, I couldn't get pregnant by Chike, maybe I could Khalil could plant his seed in me. I'll just tell Chike it's his baby. I just prayed it worked. I stared at Khalil as he sat on the sofa smoking a blunt as I sat across from him on the loveseat.

"What da fuck you looking at me for?" he asked angrily.

"Why did you choose Crue instead of me that night in the club? I was the one trying to get your attention," I asked him.

He laughed. "Shit, you should've spoke up. Both of y'all could've got it. You still want it?"

I walked over, stood in front of him and started removing my clothes. I could see his dick growing inside his grey sweats; he pulled it out and started stroking it. He licked his full, sexy lips as he watched me undress. Khalil was sexy as fuck, so I had no problem fucking him. Plus, I was feeling more secure about my body. I had always been too skinny, but since Lai gave me some weight gaining pills, my thighs had gotten thicker and my ass was plumper. Khalil's dick was black, thick and a nice length. It was nothing like Chike's but nice enough. I straddled his lap and slid down on it.

He slapped my ass cheeks. "Show me how much you been wanting this dick."

Planting my feet into the sofa cushions, I started gliding up and down on his dick until I felt the wetness slipping out of my pussy. He cupped my breasts and started licking and sucking on them. My hips started twirling as I squeezed my walls around his dick. Low grunts and groans serenaded the room as he enjoyed the ride I was giving him. My ass twerked as my pussy sucked him in and out of my drenched hole. Reaching behind me, I fondled his balls.

"Damn, keep doing that shit. Just like that," he moaned as he laid his head back on the sofa. He looked down to see his dick disappearing inside of me as my body rocked back and forth. Khalil gripped my ass cheeks and started pounding his dick inside of me. His groans became louder as he grew inside me. I gave him more of my juicy pussy bringing him closer to the edge.

"Fuck! I'm bout to come in this good ass pussy!" he barked. I buried his face in my breasts and started bouncing up and down, twirling round and round, sliding back and forth on his dick. My pussy walls gripped his dick as tight as I could until he couldn't stand it any longer.

"Sssshhhhit!" He roared as we exploded together. We lay there trying to catch our breath.

"Damn, I wonder if Crue's pussy is as good as yours," he said pissing me off. I was shocked he hadn't fucked Crue. She told me they hadn't had sex, but I didn't believe her. He was caking her like she had the best pussy he ever had. I got off his lap and went to the bathroom to clean myself up. When I came back into the living area, he was on the phone.

"You better be getting my money, or this bitch is dead," he said. It was obvious he was talking to Crue. I could hear Crue begging to speak to me. He finally passed me the phone.

I answered the phone sounding distressed. "Please Crue. He's going to kill me. Crue, I'm so scared."

"I'm sorry, Quay. I promise I'll get the money. Has he hurt you?" she asked.

"No," I said. I started to guilt her by saying her raped me, but I decided to save that lie in case I needed it later.

"I'm working on something right now. I'm trying to get the money as quick as possible," she informed me.

"I know you will. I love you, Crue," I said smiling at Khalil. He shook his head and chuckled.

"I love you too, Quay. I'm going to make this right," she promised.

"Chike has been asking about you. I don't know what to tell him. If I tell him I'm responsible for what happened, he'll tell Drek. Drek will kill me, Quay," she said with a trembling voice. I almost felt bad for putting her in this predicament, but she should've stayed away from Chike.

"Please don't tell him. I don't want anything to happen to you. Tell him, I had a family emergency. I'm going to get Khalil to let me call him, so he won't keep being suspicious," I lied. I wanted Chike to worry about me, and I wanted him to blame Crue for everything that had happened.

"That's enough of the sister bonding. Go get my money," he said before ending the call. He was smart enough to use a burner phone to call her.

"Now, come to the bedroom. I want some more of that pussy," he said standing up. *I might as well enjoy the time I'm here.*

Jedrek

"She's still stable, but unconscious. All her vitals are great. Right now, all we can do is pray for her and Zelda," Aunt Dee said over the phone.

I didn't feel comfortable leaving Vonna alone with Drekia. All it took was a phone call to Aunt Dee, and she was on Bull's private plane within a couple of hours headed to Switzerland. I was happy to hear that Drekia's surgery went well. Once she woke up, we would know if the procedure corrected the damage to her brain. I didn't care if it didn't. The only thing that mattered to me was that my sister was still alive. My heart and mind were in two places at one time. I was sitting beside Zelda praying for her to wake up. Her heart rate was so weak.

I needed to be in the streets trying to find out who did this, but I couldn't force myself to leave her side. It felt like déjà vu. The same way I wasn't there for Drekia, I wasn't there for Zelda. I was supposed to be there to protect her and Lil J.

Her parents sat in the room with me observing their baby girl. Lil J couldn't come in the ICU room, so he was with Vanity and Echon. Once again, a world of guilt rested on my shoulders. My brain was on overload trying to imagine what enemy I created that would come at her like this. I was waiting for Chike to report back to me. I didn't want to see him until he had some information for me.

"Have you eaten today?" Zelda's mom, Crystal, asked me. I hadn't eaten anything since I'd gotten back. My stomach was a bundle of bubble guts, and food was the last thing on my mind. All my time was spent by Zelda's bed side.

"Tony, take him down to the cafeteria and make him eat something. He's no good for my daughter and grandson if he's not healthy," she said to her husband.

Tony shrugged his shoulders at me. "The Queen of the family has spoken. I advise you not to argue with her."

I looked at Zelda debating whether I should leave from her side. Crystal assured me she would call my phone if need be. Tony and I took the elevator down to the first floor and into the cafeteria. I didn't realize how hungry I was until I smelled the food. I wanted to get our food and go back to Zelda's room, but Tony insisted we sit in the cafeteria and eat. We ate in silence until he spoke.

"I see that look in your eyes. You are struggling with revenge and guilt. I know because I've been where you are, son," he explained.

"How?" I asked.

"I've made my millions by protecting drug cartels, with that comes enemies. My family's lives were always at risk. Even though I'm out of the game, there are always enemies lurking. Crystal was kidnapped once in order to get me to throw a case for one of my defendants. I thank God I was able to get her back, but the guilt and hurt nearly tore us apart. All I'm saying is don't dwell on should've, would've, and could've. Those aren't the three things you need to focus on. Give your mind tunnel vision on loving and supporting Zee and Lil J, and finding the mothafucka that harmed my baby girl. Guilt ain't gon' fix nothing. It's only going to tear you down," he told me.

This wasn't the speech I expected from him. I'd been waiting for them to blame me for what happened to Zelda and to tell me they didn't want me anywhere near Zelda. I was glad that wasn't the conversation we had.

Whoever did this would pay for what they did. The security monitor only showed two masked men entering the house from the front door. Whoever it was obviously had the security code. It couldn't have been anyway from the party, because the code had been changed. It had to be someone working at the security firm I'd purchased. I vetted and kept most of the workers when I bought the place. I had Chike staking a few of the employees out to see how they moved. I was getting agitated because he hadn't reported back to me with any useful information. There was only one person that I knew had animosity with Zelda and that was her ex, Xavier. He didn't seem like the type to do anything like this, but I wasn't leaving any stones unturned.

"I need to handle a couple of things. I should be back in a few hours," I told Tony.

"Do whatever you need to do. We'll be here with her," he said nodding his head at me. I called Chike and told him to deliver Xavier to me at my hotel.

*****

I was on top of the roof at my hotel waiting for them. When Chike and Quan arrived with him, he looked like a scared little boy. I didn't have time to waste. Chike and Quan flipped him upside down, holding on to his ankles while he hung over the ledge. He instantly started pleading for his life and saying he was sorry for what he had done.

Dropping him from the roof didn't seem like punishment enough for what he did to Zelda.

"Man, I'm sorry. I know it was a punk move. Zelda got me to drop the charges. Why are you doing this shit?" He cried.

"Man, I'm bout to drop this nigga. He done shitted on his self," Chike said angrily. I wanted to laugh but held it inside.

"Pull him up," I told them. I knew the nigga didn't have anything to do with Zelda getting shot. I just needed to take my anger out on somebody. I didn't have any enemies, so I chose him.

"This nigga need a cleaning out. He stank as fuck!" Quan said looking like he was going to vomit.

"Stay the fuck away from Zelda. The next time I'm going to let them drop yo ass. You even think about reporting this shit, you a dead man. Now, get da fuck out my face," I warned him. He ran to the door that led to the inside of the building.

I stared at Chike. "Give me something. Somebody gotta know something about this. Mothafuckas know who

Zelda is to me. She's also made a name for herself. I want the person that did this before the cops find them."

"I got a couple of leads. I'm checking them out tonight. I'll have something for you tomorrow," he said with certainty. I didn't doubt his word. I wanted to give him time to handle this while I sat by Zelda's side. He was the one I wanted to take my place in a couple of years. If he could handle this, he had the spot.

"Whatever you find out, don't make any moves. Bring the information to me. I will handle it from there," I instructed him. He nodded his head. They left me standing on the roof in my thoughts.

"Yeah, what you found out?" I asked, answering the phone for Echon a few minutes later.

"He's clean. I've tracked his calls on that day. Nothing suspicious came up," he said referring to Quan. He was Chike's man. Not mine. Therefore, I didn't trust him. I was hoping it wasn't him for Chike's sake. Because if Quan was the one, that shot Zelda, Chike would have to die too.

"And the workers?" I asked.

"All clean," he replied.

"A'ight. Chike said he has a couple of things to check out. I'm going to see what he comes up with before I start spilling blood," I told Echon.

"Think strategic not with your emotions," he advised me.

He was the one that stopped me from going on a killing spree with I returned. I was ready to go to war with everyone I ever had beef with. He made me realized my energy and time needed to be focused on Zelda, Lil J and Drekia, so I fell back. The two most important women in my life were fighting for their lives. I didn't know how much longer I could hold all this aggression in.

I quickly answered my phone when I saw Crystal's phone number. I let out a deep breath when she told me Zelda was awake. Without further thought, I hurried to the hospital.

Zelda

My body felt like it weighed a ton of cement, my mouth was as dry as the Sahara Dessert, and my throat was in severe pain from the tube in my mouth. For some strange reason it felt like I had been living in a beautiful dream that instantly turned into a terrifying nightmare. I was hooked to more machines than I could count. Every sound inside the room was making my head throb, and I could barely open my eyes. Finally, I looked around at everyone until I saw Mama holding Lil J. Everyone was by my bedside, even Yella Boy and Zuri were there, but the one other person I was looking for was nowhere in sight.

Suddenly, Jedrek came rushing into the room. One of the machines started beeping liking crazy, and the nurse rushed inside the room and ordered everyone to leave out. Of course, Jedrek wasn't listening to a damn word she had to say.

"Sir, you have to leave the room with everyone else," the white, petite nurse told him.

"Make me," he said and folded his arms.

"Sir, please," she pleaded with him. It was obvious he made her nervous.

"Focus on her not me. That's yo damn job, so do it," he demanded.

She anxiously did as she was told. He stood at the foot of the bed while the nurse examined me. After she examined me, she looked at me and smiled.

"Just too much excitement. We're going to have to limit your visitors to two at a time. The doctor will be in to check up on you in a few minutes," she informed me.

I wanted to say thank you to her, but the tube in my mouth wouldn't let me. After she left the room, Jedrek walked over and sat beside my bed. A storm of emotions spiraled through my body. I was so elated to see him, but at the same time everything started replaying in my mind. I was so thankful and blessed to be alive because I truly thought I was going to die alone in my house. The only thing I could think to do was pray to God to save me. I didn't realize I was crying until Jedrek wiped the tears that slid down the sides of my face.

"Try to relax. Just lay here and rest," Jedrek told me, holding my hand. I wanted to relax but all the memories kept flashing in my head.

When I walked into my house, something felt off. I was in such a hurry to get back to Vanity's house since she was watching Lil J that I ignored the gut feeling inside me. If I had taken heed, I would've left back out as soon as I entered. I went straight to my office to get the files I needed. As I was going through my file cabinet, I heard voices coming down the hall. I reached for my phone to call 911 but realized I didn't have it. I wanted to knock myself in the head for leaving it in the car. EJ's bat was lying in the corner of the room, so I grabbed it and hid behind the door.

As soon as they walked into the office, I clobbered one of them in the head with the bat, and he fell to the floor. Unfortunately, when I swung at the other one, he blocked the bat with his arm. After snatching the bat away from me, he grabbed hold of my arm. I started screaming and kicking like a wild cat. I pulled the mask off his face to see a man I'd never seen before. When I kicked him in the groin, he let me go. I made a quick dash for the door, but the other one grabbed my ankle causing me to fall. I kicked him hard in the face, then grabbed the bat that was lying on the floor and started swinging on them. They got tired of defending themselves from my blows.

The next thing I heard was a gunshot. My adrenaline was pumping so fast, I didn't feel the pain. It took a few seconds to realize I had been shot. When I looked down to see the blood seeping through my blouse, I felt the excruciating pain. My body became weak and I collapsed on the floor. The next thing I remember was Crue trying to help me.

With everything that happened, I forgot about Drekia's surgery. I knew she survived the surgery or Jedrek wouldn't be here. He would probably be in Switzerland trying to kill Dr. Abei. I reached up to snatch the tube from my mouth, but Jedrek grabbed my wrist.

"Da fuck you doing?" he asked angrily. I tried to talk, but he couldn't understand anything I was saying. "Just chill out until the doctor comes in here. I'm going to ask you some questions. All I want you to do is nod your head yes or no," he said. I nodded my head.

"Do you know who did this or why?" he asked. I shook my head no. I didn't have any enemies. I was a criminal lawyer, but I didn't recall being threatened by anyone. I hadn't had a client yet that hadn't been satisfied with the way I had handled their case.

"Have you ever seen them before?" he asked his next question.

I shook my head again. I glanced at him to see his mind turning. I knew he thought it was someone who was after him, and that could be a possibility, but I didn't want him going through that guilt. There was so much I wanted to say to him but couldn't because of the tube down my throat. I was getting impatient waiting on the doctor. I tried sitting up in the bed, but Jedrek gave me a look that told me to lie there. I was sure this was some of Quan's friends that came back to rob me. Crue must've gave Quan my security code. I prayed that was not the case, but I couldn't think of anyone that would want to harm me. I was happy to see the doctor come into the room. This was my first time seeing the woman who saved my life.

"Happy to see you are awake. It's nice to finally meet you, Zelda. I'm Dr. Kelton," she said smiling at me. She was an average looking, petite, white woman with sandy brown hair. I pointed at the tube in my mouth letting her know I wanted it out.

"I will have the nurse come in and remove it as soon as I'm done examining you," she said. Jedrek sat texting on his phone while Dr. Kelton examined me. He didn't see the concerned look on her face when she looked at my heart rate. I didn't think she noticed me look. I wasn't a doctor, but I'd seen that same worry in Vanity's eyes. Vanity always got a gloomy look when she had to send a patient to a specialist.

"You will definitely be here for a couple of weeks at least. We gotta get that heart rate up and blood pressure normal," she said trying to sound optimistic. I wasn't buying any of her shit. I knew something was wrong with me. I guess she didn't want to stress me in my condition.

"How's everything looking with her?" Jedrek asked with concern.

"Everything is looking good. Your heart rate is improving," she said forcing a smile. I decided to let her have that lie for now. The last thing I wanted to do was add more stress to Jedrek's overwhelmed mind. I pointed to her pen and notepad that was in her white coat.

"You wanna write something?" she asked me. I nodded my head. After she passed the pen and notepad, I wrote Jedrek a note to go get Lil J. He kissed me on the forehead before leaving the room. I quickly scribbled a note to Dr. Kelton.

DO NOT discuss my condition with anyone but me

She nodded her head. "There's no need to be concerned right now. There's too much swelling and fluid around your heart so your body needs time to heal. After that, we will know more about the condition of your heart. I'm sure we can get that all under control while you are here. We can talk more about it tomorrow. Please don't stress. It's nothing we can't handle. Dr. Bailon is a heart specialist, I'm going to have him monitoring your heart while I monitor everything else."

Before she left, I wrote another note:

Thank you for saving me

She gave me a wide smile and exited the room.

Two Days Later

Crue

I had four days to save Quay's life, and I only had five hundred dollars. I had been scoping potential niggas I could finesse or rob for the money. Atlanta was full of a lot of capping ass niggas. They looked like they had money but were broke as hell. I have two options left: I could go crawling back to Quan or Gerard. That still wouldn't get me the money, because neither of them was going to come off a hundred grand for me. Not even if I told them it was to save Quay's life. I thought of telling Chike, but I knew he would tell Jedrek. Quay would live, but I'd be dead. Plus, Jedrek would probably kill Chike for not telling him about the run in we had with Khalil. I knew the code to Quan's safe, so I decided to try my luck with him.

I was parked down the street from Quan's house. I didn't see his car, so I made my way to the back door of the house. I still had a key, but I broke the backdoor window, because he would know it was me if I let myself in. I made my way to the closet in the bathroom. The safe was built in behind all his clothes hanging in the closet. I smiled to myself when I opened the safe; it was full of money. His stingy ass was giving me pennies while he had over a hundred grand.

I was going to take as much as the bag could hold. He'd regret buying that bitch a car and not me. Just as I was stuffing the last stack of bills in my bag someone yanked me by my hair causing me to scream out in pain. My body went flying across the room and slammed against the bedroom dresser. I looked up and stared into the eyes of Quan, who looked more like a raging bull.

"Bitch, you come back to steal from me?" he roared with spit flying from his mouth. He picked me up off the floor by my neck. Tears instantly started to fall down my face; I knew he was going to kill me. He bitch slapped me causing blood to spill from my mouth, then he threw me on the bed. My back ached from being thrown against the dresser. Quan yanked me off the bed by my ankle, and my head hit the floor with a thud. I kicked and screamed as he pulled me out of the bedroom.

"Man, what da fuck going on?" Chike said rushing inside the house.

"Caught this trifling bitch trying to steal from my stash!" Quan told him. He was still holding on to my ankle, and I was kicking and squirming to get away from him.

Chike looked down at me with a malicious look on his face. They were going to kill me together. Quan started dragging me again.

"Where da fuck you going with her?" Chike asked, angrily.

"Put this bitch in the trunk. I'm gon' kill her hoe ass. The bitch was pregnant with another nigga baby anyway. Trifling ass got an abortion," Quan spewed with venom.

"Man, let her go," Chike said.

"Nigga, didn't you hear me say the bitch tried to steal from me?" Quan asked him.

"But she didn't. You did enough. Let her go," Chike demanded. He wasn't asking Quan to release me; it was an order. Quan released my ankle with force and stepped in Chike's face.

"You wanna tell me something, brotha?" Quan asked. It was obvious he was asking Chike was he fucking me.

Chike chuckled and eyed him down. "Brotha, I'm saving your life. That's Zelda's cousin. If you kill her, what you think Jedrek gon' do to you?"

"How he gon' find out?" Quan asked him, insinuating Chike would snitch on him. The room was quiet for a few seconds. Quan stormed out the living room and into the bedroom. Chike walked over to me and kneeled beside me. He pulled out his gun and put it to my temple. I said a quick prayer knowing this was the end of my life.

"Take yo ass straight to Mama's house. If you make me come look for you, I will end you. You gon' tell me what da fuck going on or you will be explaining some shit to Jedrek. Now, get da fuck out before I let Quan deal with you," he demanded in a low voice. He didn't have to tell me twice. I hurried my aching body out of the house.

*****

"My got damn son sho' know how to pick 'em. Get yo ass in here," Shyma said shaking her head. I walked into her house with my head down.

"Chike told me to come over and wait for him," I mumbled. I kept my head down, because I didn't want her to see my busted lip. She walked over to me with her hand on her hip. Shyma placed her hand under my chin and lifted my head.

"Chile, you need to slow yo wild ass down. One of these niggas is gon' kill you about they money," she said staring at me. I was embarrassed to know he told his mom what I tried to do.

"Go into the den and sit down. I'll get some ice for that lip. You gon' be looking like Bubba from *Forrest Gump* in the morning," she said walking away. I went into the den and flopped down on the sofa. All I could do was let out a soft cry as I made up my mind I was going to tell Jedrek what I did. It was the only way to save Quay's life.

"Here chile," Shyma said passing me the Ziploc bag filled with ice before she sat down and started watching television. I supposed Krysta was with her mother. I sat there a few minutes, and decided it was time to face my fate. The longer I waited the worse it was going to get.

"Thank you for letting me come here, but I'm going to leave. I have some personal matters I need to handle. Tell Chike I'm going to tell Jedrek. He'll know what I mean," I said standing up.

"Nah I don't know what da fuck that means," Chike said walking into the den.

"That's my cue to leave. I'm going to pick up Krysta. I'll be back in a couple of hours," Shyma said standing up and walking out the den. I waited until I heard the front door close. I wasn't going to go up against Chike and Shyma.

"I'm leaving too," I said standing up.

"And do what? Try to rob another nigga. Zelda is laying in the hospital with a bullet hole in her chest. Quay damn missing and you trying to secure a damn lick? You pathetic as fuck. You ain't even been to see Zelda since you went ghost the night she was shot."

"You don't know shit about what I'm going through! Get out of my way," I said walking up to him.

"I see you one of those selfish ass females. I should've let Quan body yo ass," he said with evilness in his mean eyes.

"I didn't ask you to save me." I didn't care if he did save my life. He had no right to talk down on me.

"You are the worst type of woman. You think you out here finessing niggas, but all you getting is pocket change from niggas. Quan scoped you out on day one. Niggas smell a female like you a mile away, and they don't mind throwing a few dollars for a good piece of ass. That's all you worth to them. You'll never be the female that gets the ring, family, house and cars. You'll always have your legs in the air for bread. Just like a bird. Duck pussy is all you are," he spit at me with venom in his voice.

His words hurt more than they should. I shouldn't have cared about his opinion of me. But hearing him say such awful things about me hurt deep. Maybe because everything he said was the truth. I had been chasing money and using men for so long, I didn't see I was the one getting used up by them. They never had any intentions of making me anything more than a good fuck. His words hurt, but the tears flowing down my face angered me. I never wanted to show weakness to a man.

"Fuck you! You don't know anything about me! I don't need or want your help with anything. I'll chance losing my life with Jedrek," I said trying to walk past him.

"No da fuck you won't!" He said grabbing my arm.

"Let me go!" I screamed trying to yank away from him.

"Jedrek don't need shit else on his plate. Fucked up as his mind is right now, he won't give your life a second thought before he ends it. Now, tell me what the fuck is going on," he demanded. He was the only hope I had of getting Quay out of this mess alive, so I broke down and told him everything that Khalil had done.

Chike

"Sit down." I wanted to kill her myself for the mess she'd caused, but something inside me had a weakness for her. She walked over and sat down on the sofa with her head down. I sat across from her on the loveseat.

"When's the last time you talked to Quay?" I asked calmly. There was no point in showing her how mad I was. It was obvious she was beating herself up about this.

"The other day. She's so scared. You don't know Khalil. If I don't come up with that money, he will kill her and then come for me. I'm the reason Zelda is laying up in that hospital. I haven't been back to see her because I feel like shit," she said remorsefully.

"So, you was gon' fuck a hundred grand out of niggas in seven days?" I asked angrily.

"I didn't spill my guts to you for you to throw it in my face. And I don't fuck every man I finesse. Some niggas just give freely," she spat back at me.

"Call him and tell him you got the money," I told her.

"You're going to pay it for Quay?" She asked surprised and excited.

"No, I'm going to kill him," I replied bluntly.

Her eyes grew big. It wasn't that I wouldn't pay the money for Quay. I just knew how this shit worked. Khalil wasn't going to let her, or Quay walk away after he got the money. He would kill them. I couldn't believe she was going to try and do this all on her own. I respected her courage but wanted to cuss her out for being naïve. I asked her as many questions as I could about Khalil. I had gotten the license plate of the rental he was driving when he showed up at the abortion clinic. Genius was the man to find the car in Atlanta, but I didn't have direct contact to him.

Jedrek always reached out to him when we needed information. There was only one other person I knew that had direct contact to him. I would make up a lie to Echon to get the information I needed. It wasn't that I didn't trust Echon, I just didn't want him to have to keep secrets from Jedrek. I wasn't scared to tell Jedrek what was going on, but he needed to keep his mind focused on his family. This was a distraction he didn't need; plus, he left this situation with me to handle. Crue pulled her cellphone from her back pocket. It wasn't until then that I noticed how nervous and scared she was. Her hand was shaking as she tried to dial the phone number. I went and sat beside her taking the phone from her hand.

"Take a deep breath. We gon' get her back. I gotchu," I said confidently.

She stared at me with concerned eyes. That feeling hit me when I saw the soft side of her. There was a side to her that only a few witnessed. A part that made me think the forbidden. It felt like everything that was happening in the world stopped as we sat there staring at each other. My dick started to grow inside my boxers. The only thing that stopped me from sucking her tongue into my mouth was the busted lip that Quan caused. I stood up to break the trance she had on me.

"Here. Call him," I said giving her the phone. She took a deep breath and dialed the number. I sat back down on the loveseat across from her and listened.

"Yea, you got my money," Khalil said answering the phone.

"Yea, please just tell me where to bring it, so you can let Quay go," she pleaded with him. Crue had mad love for her friend. She was going to risk her own life to save Quay.

Any other female would've just skipped town and prayed for the best.

"I'll find it. I promise I'll be alone. Just please don't hurt her," she pleaded after a brief pause. "Can I speak...hello?" she said. Khalil had ended the call before she could speak with Quay.

"When we meeting him?" I asked eagerly.

"Tomorrow night. He said he will text me the address thirty minutes before we meet," she said. I was hoping to get the place of the meet, but he was smart to prepare for a setup. I needed to think of how I was going to save Crue and Quay. I needed Genius to locate Khalil's rental car before tomorrow night. The only way I could do that was to reach out to Echon.

"I have to go handle something. Go to the hospital and visit Zelda. She's awake. Come back here when you leave the hospital," I told her as I stood up. Her eyes lit up when I told her Zelda was awake. She stood up with me.

"I'm serious, Crue. Bring yo ass back here. Don't do no dumb shit," I warned her.

"I will and I won't. Where are you going? When will you be back?" she asked.

The look in her eyes showed concern for me. I know I shouldn't, but my body was reacting on its own. I walked over and grazed her bruised lip with my thumb. She closed her eyes with her mouth slightly gaped. When she opened her eyes, my eyes were still glued to her face.

"This can only happen once," she said softly closing her eyes.

Once was all I needed to get her out of my system. I picked her up wrapping her legs around me. She wrapped her arms around my neck while licking and kissing on my neck. My dick started pounding from the wetness of her tongue against my skin. I carried her down the hall to the bedroom. After lying her on the bed, she gazed up at me. Nothing was telling me this was wrong. I needed to know she was sure this was what she wanted also.

"You sure about this?" She sat up and pulled her blouse over her head and removed her bra. I let out a slight grunt admiring her perky breasts. She kept her eyes focused on me as she removed her shoes and jeans. Her pussy was completely bald, the way I loved it. She laid back down and watched me undress. Her eyes trailed down to my hard dick that was throbbing and aching. Her eyes were full of nervousness and lust. When I laid on top of her, the head of my dick pressed against her entrance. Her body shivered when my tongue licked the dark circles around her breasts, and my teeth gently bit on her hard nipples. She let out soft, sexy moans as her hands caressed my back. Her hips started twirling and I could feel my dick slipping in and out of her wet pussy. I licked, sucked and bit her breast until her soft moans turned into cries of pleasure. I had no plans of eating her pussy, but I was on a sexual high. I wanted to feel and taste every part of her. I licked my way down until she stopped me.

"No, that's too personal," she said looking down at me. I wanted this to be as personal as it could be, but I wasn't going to force anything on her. With an arch in my back, I lay on top of her. She planted the soles of her feet into the bed spreading her legs wide. I could feel her heart pounding against my chest. She gripped my ass and lift her hips. My dick slowly slid inside her soaking wet, warm, tight-as-fuck pussy.

"Sssshhhhit!" I roared feeling precum ooze from me. I quickly pulled out of her and gripped my mushroom head. I didn't expect her pussy to feel this damn good. Crue wrapped her legs around my waist and stroked my abs. Her eyes pleaded with me to relieve the sexual tension between us. I slid back inside her trying to think of things that would distract me. Her walls were gripping my dick and sucking me in. Pussy juice was spilling from her like a cracked dam I could feel it splatter on my thighs. I drove my aching dick deeper and harder inside. Her fingernails dug into my back as she moaned with ecstasy. My hips started winding and when I found her spot, I jabbed my dick against it repeatedly. Her sexual aroma was an aphrodisiac. I wanted to taste the juice that was pouring from her. My arms cupped her legs pushing them in the air making me glide deeper inside her and pressing against her wetness.

"Ooooohhhh my God! I'm commmminnngg!" she screamed. Her body stiffened and trembled as her eyes rolled to the back of her head. Something about watching her come made me crazy.

"Fuuuccck!" I barked as I started ramming my dick inside of her with no mercy. For everything I started giving her, she gave me more back. She started throwing her pussy on me, driving me insane. Her pussy walls held on to my shaft like her life depended on it. She started coming back to back and making me fuck her harder. I was so caught up in watching her come, I came with her and kept going. I flipped over on my back to watch her ride me. She looked like a beautiful, chocolate muse riding my dick. Splashing wet sounds were overheard with her moans and whimpers. I massaged her breasts and pinched her nipples and she bounced on my dick. Her ass cheeks jiggled and slapped against my thighs.

"I'm 'bout to come again," she cried out throwing her head back. I gripped her hips and started slamming her down on me. My toes locked up and my abs cramped up.

"Aaaarrggghhh Fuuuucckkkk!" I roared like a beast as we came together. Her sweaty body collapsed against my chest. She trembled as her orgasm ripped through her. I could feel her walls contracting around my soft dick that was still inside her. We lay there quiet. She would quiver every time my dick jumped inside her.

"You better get up unless you want more," I advised her. I was hoping for another round. She slowly got up and the room filled with awkwardness. She went to the bathroom without looking at me. I sat on side of the bed wondering if one time was going to be enough. A few minutes later, she came out. I stood up to see her staring at the bed. Her juices saturated the entire bed.

"I need to shower," she said still looking at the drenched bed.

"Go ahead. I'll use the other one," I told her. She quickly hurried back into the bathroom. I went to the extra bathroom to shower.

I was in the den texting Echon when she walked in the den. Neither one of us looked at each other. It felt weird, but I didn't regret what happened. I just didn't know how to handle things between us now. We jumped when we heard the front door opening. I could hear Krysta's little feet running down the hall. When she entered the den, she didn't run to me. She ran over and hugged Crue's legs. Crue giggled and leaned down giving Krysta a warm hug. Krysta cried when Crue told her she had to leave. She wouldn't stop until I told her Crue would be back later, and she could stay up until she came back. Mama rolled her eyes. After Crue left, Ma kept giving me a side eye.

"What Ma?" I asked.

"Ain't you fucking her best friend, and she's fucking yo best friend?" she asked in a low voice.

"It ain't even like that between me and Quay," I said.

I knew what things were like between Quay and me. I didn't know what this thing was developing between Crue and me. But I did know she was off limits to me from this point on. Even if she wasn't, Crue had too much growing up to do. I was trying to raise my daughter; and trying to get Special to get her life together was enough. I didn't have the energy to put into Crue's bullshit.

Quay

I knew Crue would get the money; now my mind was on what I was going to do with my share. Khalil and Mikah were discussing places for the drop off and my patience with them was running thin. I didn't understand why they wanted to meet in a secluded place. To me, it would be better to meet in a public area. The only good thing about being around them was sex with Khalil. He had some good sex, but he wasn't Chike. Chike was the type of man a woman wants to build a life with. Khalil was just a fuck buddy type of nigga.

"If Crue went to Jedrek for help, it's best to meet in a public area. A secluded area gives him a better chance of killing you," I suggested.

"Why da fuck you keep talking about that nigga? That fool can bleed just like me. Shut da fuck up," Khalil said angrily. I rolled my eyes at him.

"Hey, ain't that the name of the nigga that killed Maniac? What he look like?" Mikah asked nudging Khalil's arm. Khalil looked at me with murder in his eyes.

"Bitch, you trying to set me up?" he asked angrily, walking toward me with his hand balled up into a fist. I scooted in the corner of the sofa.

"No! Why would you think that? I don't even know anyone name Maniac. Who is that?" I asked frightened.

"My damn uncle. What that Jedrek nigga look like?" Khalil asked. I gave him the best description of Jedrek that I could.

"Yea, that's him," Mikah said nodding his head.

"Did he used to play football?" Khalil asked me.

"Yea, I remember Zelda saying something about his knee injury stopped him from going Pro. That's all I know. I don't know anything about him killing anyone," I told them.

"Yea, I hope he does show up. I get my money and I get to kill his bitch ass," Khalil said nodding his head at Mikah. I didn't want anyone to die; I just wanted things to work out for me, just once.

"We need to be prepared for this. You're the only one they're expecting. I can be in the cut ready to take him out first chance I get," Mikah said.

Khalil nodded his head. "Yea, that black mothafucka gon' finally get his. Go find the perfect place."

This was almost over. I couldn't wait to get back and start my life with Chike. Ever since I met him, I dreamed of having a family with him. If that meant being a mother to his daughter, I'd try my best. But if I was going to play mother, the birth mother needed to go. Since I would be doing her job, she didn't need to be in our lives. I prayed all this worked out the way I wanted. I didn't want Jedrek to get killed. Khalil and Mikah were the only two that I didn't care whether they lived or died.

Khalil sat on the sofa and fired up a blunt. He tried passing it to me, but I declined. I'd been drug free for the past month, and I wanted my life with Chike. In order to have that, I knew I had to leave the drugs alone. Crue thought I had a problem with drugs, but I didn't. I only did drugs, because they took me out of my awkward shyness. When I was high, I felt sexy, desired and carefree. I was a fun person when I was high. Now, I had Chike to have fun with.

"Why did Jedrek kill your uncle?" I asked Khalil.

"The bitch ass nigga didn't kill him. He slaughtered him. My uncle's body parts were discovered in several different places in Atlanta. My ol' man was killed when I was three. Maniac was the only family I had; he took care of me. After he was killed, I moved from foster home to foster home. I always said I wanted to kill the nigga that took my uncle from me. This is my chance," he explained.

"But *why* did he kill him?" I asked again. Jedrek was crazy, but he wasn't the type to kill someone without just cause.

"It don't got damn matter, bitch. You trying to take up for the nigga?" he asked angrily, jumping up from the couch. Khalil was a woman beater. He proved that last night when we were fucking. I called out Chike's name and he whooped my ass. He didn't leave any marks on my face, but my left side was bruised from him kicking me. Another ass whooping wasn't what I wanted, so I decided to calm him down. I sat on the edge of the couch and smiled up at him. I sucked him off until he squirted his semen on my face. He took me to the bedroom and fucked me until Mikah came back.

"Yo, I found a place," Mikah said banging on the bedroom door. Khalil slipped on a pair of sweats and walked out the room. A few minutes later, he walked back into the bedroom and told me to get dressed so I could ride with them to check out the spot Mikah chose for the drop.

*****

"Quaysha!" A hometown voice called out my name as we walked through the hotel lobby. I looked over my shoulder and saw Amy. She was one of the popular girls I hung with for a little while. They only used me because I had a car, but I didn't care. It wasn't that I wasn't popular in school. I just wasn't one of those girls that everyone wanted to be around. I was just one of those girls that everyone knew because the city we lived in was small as hell. Amy also knew I lied about them recording me against my will. Her and two other girls made the entire school hate me for lying. I still never admitted that I was lying; I stuck to my lie. Most people believed me, but they were too scared to go against Amy and her crew. Eventually they turned the entire school against me.

"Hi Amy," I said dryly. She looked at Khalil and Mikah.

She smiled at me. "You still making videos. I at least hope you getting paid for it now."

"Come on. We ain't got time for a class reunion," Khalil said pulling me away. I couldn't wait to go back home and rub my life with Chike in everyone's faces.

Zelda

Crue started crying the moment she walked into my room. The worried look on her face reminded me that she said she needed to talk to me about something. She had called me as I drove to my house the day I was shot. I reached out for her to come beside my bed. I was feeling better than I was yesterday, but I felt in my gut that something was wrong with me. My heart rate still was weak, and nurses came in every hour to monitor my heart rate and blood pressure. Jedrek slept in the recliner and jumped up every time a nurse came into the room. I had to force him to leave this morning so he could get some sleep. Lil J was staying with my parents at his house, because Jedrek didn't want them staying at my house. I didn't think I would ever stay there again. My home didn't feel like the safe, peaceful place that I loved so much anymore. Crue walked over by my bed and held my hand.

"Stop crying," I said in a froggy voice. The nurse had removed the breathing tube, but my throat was sore.

"I hate seeing you in here like this," she said wiping away her tears.

"I know, but you saved my life. If you hadn't come, I wouldn't be here now. Thank you," I said smiling at her.

"Are you going to be okay?" she asked worriedly.

"Yea," I said with false confidence. As a lawyer, I had perfected my poker face.

"I'm so sorry. I should be the one in here, not you," she said remorsefully.

"Stop it. I don't want to talk about this. How are you doing?" I asked not wanting to think about the hot lead burning into my flesh on the day I was shot.

"You don't understand Zee. This is…," she said before I cut her off.

"Crue, that day was horrific. If you don't mind, I would much rather talk about what was on your mind that day. You called me wanting to talk about something," I told her feeling emotional.

"It was nothing," she said. I could tell she had something on her mind. There was a glimmer in her eyes, but I could always see sadness.

"I know I haven't been the best role model for you since you've been here. I was so focused on my own life that I neglected you. I'm sorry for that. I want you to know you can talk to me about anything," I told her. She sat down in the chair beside my bed and dropped her head.

"No matter how hard I try to do the right things to have a good life, I always do something wrong," she said.

"What did you do?" I asked. She glanced up at me with her eyes full of guilt. They were pleading for me to be understanding. I had too much experience with guilty clients, so I knew the look very well.

"You ever found yourself being attracted to one of Vanity's boyfriends?" she asked. I knew exactly where she was going with this.

"Chike?" I asked. She dropped her head again.

"Look at me, Crue," I said to her. I pushed the button to raise my bed as she looked up at me.

"No, I've never been attracted to any of Vanity's boyfriends. I've only known two of them. The first one I didn't like, and Echon ain't right in the head," I said smiling at her.

"Neither is Jedrek," she said seriously. I laughed.

"No, but there's always that something that draws you to a person. I didn't want to feel anything for Jedrek. I fought it for as long as I could. So, did he. Does Chike know you feel this way?" I asked. The look on her face told me everything.

"How far has it gone between you and him?" I asked.

"I promise it only happened once, and it will never happen again," she said as if she needed to convince me. I knew she was only trying to convince herself.

"You have to be honest with yourself, Crue. Something tells me this is more than sex you are feeling," I told her.

She stood up in frustration. "I don't know what it is. I couldn't stand him. These feelings just came from nowhere."

"I'm going to be honest with you. This could cost you the friendship you have with Quay. I haven't met a man yet that I would give up my friendship with Vanity for. That includes Jedrek. Think about what's most important to you. You have to choose between your friendship with Quay and what you are feeling for Chike," I advised her.

"I don't want to talk about this anymore. Can we talk about something else?" she asked flopping back down in the chair. I didn't want to talk about being shot, so I asked her about styling my hair in some box plaits. She agreed to come back in a couple of days to do it for me. My hair was getting tangled since it was wild and bushy on my head. Only black women were bold enough to have their hair done while lying up in a hospital. The rest of our conversation was about her taking her gift for braiding hair more serious. I agreed to help build her brand in any way I could. Dr. Kelton walked into the room with a short, stocky, man with skin color as brown as mine. He had to be the heart doctor she mentioned. Crue said she had some things to handle and gave me a tight hug before leaving and promising to come back tomorrow.

"How are you feeling?" Dr. Kelton asked with a smile.

"Better," I said.

"Good. Well, this is Dr. Bailon. He's the heart doctor that will be monitoring your heart for the rest of your stay here," she said glancing at Dr. Bailon. I gave him a half smile.

"You don't have to be scared of me," he said walking closer to my bed.

"I'm not scared of you. I'm frightened about what you are here to tell me," I confessed to him. He sat down in the chair that Crue had occupied. Dr. Kelton stood at the foot of my bed with her hands in her white coat.

"I'm one of the best, so you are in good hands," he said winking at me. I forced a smile.

"Why isn't my heart rate getting better?" I asked wanting to hear the truth.

He cleared his throat and looked at me. "The bullet damaged some of your arteries. We are going to go in and correct as much damage as we can." He rambled on about the procedure, but it was like he was talking in a hole. I was in my early thirties and having heart surgery. This wasn't supposed to be my life. I had just had my baby and fell in love with the man I wanted to spend the rest of my life with. I sat quietly as he kept talking.

"Will I be able to live a normal life?" I asked him.

"Absolutely. You are a healthy young woman. The complications to your heart aren't due to your health. The bullet damaged some of your arteries. It's causing your heart muscles to do more work. I've done this type of surgery numerous times, Ms. Vandross," he said smiling at me.

"When?" I asked.

"In a couple of days," he said. He started talking medical talk about the muscles being overworked. All I could think about was seeing Lil J and Jedrek. The worst possibilities started running through my mind, and the heart monitor started going crazy. My throat felt like it was closing.

"Breath Zelda. You are having a panic attack," Dr. Kelton said rushing to the other side of the bed. I needed to talk to Vanity. She was the optimist; I was the pessimist. I needed her to tell me everything was going to be okay.

"Take deep breaths and try to relax," Dr. Bailon instructed me. They stayed with me until I calmed down. Dr. Bailon said he would be by later today to check on me. After they left my room, I grabbed my cellphone that Jedrek brought to me.

"Hey, how you are feeling this morning?" Vanity asked happily.

"Are you busy?" I asked trying to hold back the tears.

"I'm at work getting ready to see a patient, but I got a minute to talk. What up?" she asked.

"I need you," I blurted out unable to hold the tears.

"I'm on my way. Stay on the phone with me. We don't have to talk about what's wrong. Let's talk about the stupid shit until I get there," she said. She started rambling about stupid things trying to make me laugh. I heard her tell her receptionist to cancel all her appointments for the day. By the time she made it to the hospital, she had me in tears laughing at corny jokes.

Crue

Seeing Zelda in the hospital made me realize how reckless I was being with my life. I always knew I was risking my life by robbing niggas, but never thought I would jeopardize the life of my family and friends. Knowing Zelda was going to be okay made me feel better. Now, I needed to help get Quay back safely. I promised myself I was going to do better with my life. Chike's words to me earlier were cruel but true; it was time for me to grow up. My heart skipped a beat thinking about him, and my pussy throbbed thinking about our time together. The man gave me the type of dick I had only seen on porn. He drilled my pussy like he was trying to strike oil. The way he looked at me when he was fucking me made me feel like I was his forever, but that wasn't true. We belonged to each other for a couple of hours.

When I pulled into Shyma's driveway, she was coming out the house with Chike and Krysta. Chike was holding Krysta in his arms, and she was holding on to him with her tiny arms wrapped around his neck. I hurried and jumped out the car.

"What's wrong? Is she okay?" I asked frantically. Chike and Shyma looked at me like I was crazy. Krysta lifted her head from Chike's chest with the biggest smile on her face. I took a deep breath relieved that she was fine.

"She's fine. She's just a daddy's girl," Shyma said nonchalantly. Chike put Krysta in the car seat inside Shyma's Mercedes Benz while Shyma got in the driver's seat.

"Be careful. We'll be back in a couple of days," she said to Chike. He nodded his head.

"If something happens to my baby, I'm coming for you," she warned me. It wasn't a threat but a promise. She loved her son as much as Chike loved Krysta. She backed out of the driveway waving bye to Chike. I followed Chike inside the house.

"Where are they going?" I asked. I followed him into the bedroom that we shared a few hours ago. Looking at the bed gave me goose bumps and chills. He didn't seem bothered by what we did. He was back to acting like I was nobody to him.

"Do you know how to shoot a gun?" he asked.

"No, why?" I asked curiously.

"You out here robbing niggas and don't know how to protect yourself?" he asked shockingly.

"I never give them a chance to get that close. I be gone by the time they realize I hit them for a lick," I boasted about my skills. The look on his face made me regret my words.

"Come on," he said walking out the bedroom. I rushed behind him following him outside to his truck.

"Where we going?" I asked getting in on the passenger's side. He ignored my question.

*****

We drove down a country road with nothing but woods for miles. At the end of the road was a big concrete building. He drove behind the building and parked. I sat in the truck as he got out and unlocked the door to the building. He never told me to come inside, but I jumped out the truck and followed him. The inside of the building was full of glass windows and window frames. It looked like a workman's shop with tables and tools everywhere.

"What's this place?" I asked looking around.

"I ain't tell yo ass to get out," he said walking over to a wall.

He punched on a keypad and the wall opened. There was a damn arsenal inside the room. A huge safe that looked like it should be in a bank's vault hung on the wall. He took a small gun off a table and walked out of the room. Like a little puppy, I followed behind him. He led me into the woods by a small lake.

"You gotta learn how to fire a gun," he said holding the gun out for me to take.

"I'm going to have to kill someone?" I asked mortified. I was a lot of things, but a killer was not one.

"I hope not, but I need you to know how to shoot if it comes to that," he said. It wasn't up for debate. I caused this mess, so I had to do whatever to correct it. I took the gun from him, and he walked over and placed some empty glass bottles on a table. He walked back over and looked at me holding the gun.

"You've never held a gun?" he asked. I shook my head and he shook his too.

"What kind of gun is this?" I asked.

"A twenty-two. It's light and doesn't pack much power," he said. He started explaining the parts of the gun and how to hold it. While he was talking, my eyes were focused on his lips. I wanted to feel them against mine.

The sun was shining bright and the Georgia heat came along with it. The woods were full of bugs flying around my head. I tried aiming at the bottles, but the bugs were distracting. I kept trying to fan them away.

"Stop waving the damn gun around! The safety ain't on," he barked, grabbing my wrist.

"How da fuck I'm supposed to know that? I've never held a gun! These damn bugs irritating me! And they biting the shit out of my legs!" I screamed back at him. I was wearing a distressed jean skirt that stopped midway on my thighs. The mosquitos were feasting on me.

"Face the table," he told me. When I turned toward the table, I could feel his presence standing close behind me. His sexy voice instructed me on how to aim at the bottles. His body was so close to mine, it made me forget about the mosquitos drinking my blood.

"I just need to know you comfortable firing a gun. Relax," he said. I couldn't relax with him standing this close to me. I could feel his dick against my lower back. I closed my eyes a shot. I quickly opened them when I heard glass shatter.

"I did it!" I screamed jumping up and down. He laughed.

"I bet your eyes were closed," he said when I turned to face him.

"So, I still shot one," I said bopping my head.

"Turn around and do it again with your eyes open," he directed me. I shot the gun until there were no more bullets, but I only hit two bottles. He reloaded the gun for me to keep practicing. After I unloaded those bullets, he loaded the gun again. By the fourth reload, I was tired of shooting.

"I'm tired," I told him when he started loading the gun again. He looked at me and stopped loading. I followed him back into the building where he put the gun back behind the wall. The heat had my body sweaty and sticky, and his fitted tee was drenched with sweat.

"Come on," he said. I got back in the truck and we headed back into the city.

"What was that place?" I asked.

"It's where I build windows. It's my side hustle," he said.

I laughed. "And selling drugs is your business?"

"Yea, until I get to the place where I can make my side hustle my business," he answered.

I had so many questions I wanted to ask him about his life, but I knew he would never share his personal life or business with me. He knew what he wanted to do with his life. I admired him for that. I didn't think he would share his personal life with me, so I asked about his business.

"You ever did anyone's home?" I asked.

"I don't install them. Just sell them. And yea I have. I made the windows for Jedrek's house," he said looking straight ahead. My mouth dropped open. Jedrek's windows in his home were beautiful.

"If you are telling the truth, you are truly talented. You can really make that a legit money maker," I told him.

"Thanks," he said glancing at me. I reached down to scratch my legs. The mosquitos had a field day with me.

"Don't scratch them. Just rub on them," he said glancing at the bumps on my thighs. We rode and talked about nothing and everything. He talked about Krysta and his mom. I talked about my parents. We shared childhood stories. Things between us started to feel different. I just knew that wasn't a good thing.

"I'm sorry," I said softly as he drove.

"For what?" he asked looking straight ahead.

"For getting you in my mess. Thank you for helping me," I told him.

"It was either help you or let you and Quay get killed," he said. I didn't have a reply for him. If Khalil didn't kill me, I still had Jedrek to worry about.

"But you welcome," he said glancing at me. I smiled at him. He chuckled and shook his head.

*****

I thought we were going back to Shyma's house, but that wasn't the direction he was going. He drove into a quiet and well-kept neighborhood, and pulled into the driveway of a moderate size, red brick house. I didn't move until he told me to get out. We walked to the front door, he unlocked it and I followed him inside. When I walked into the living room, the first thing that caught my eye was a picture of him and Krysta hanging over a fireplace. The house was decorated with black, burgundy and white furniture, pictures and knick-knacks.

"This your house?" I asked turning to face him.

"Nah, I'm just renting from Jedrek," he said pulling his shirt off. My eyes ogled his dark chocolate, ripped stomach then scanned down to his jeans that hung low revealing his perfect V.

"I went to Zelda's house to grab some clothes. My bag is in my car at Shyma's house," I told him. It gave me the creeps when I went by Zelda's house this morning. The big, beautiful home didn't feel so homely anymore. I hoped she didn't plan on returning there when she was released from the hospital.

"Go ahead and shower. I'll go get it. We need to be ready when you get the call. Grab a T-shirt and boxers out my room 'til I get back," he said. He made sure to lock the door on his way out. I gave myself a tour of the house; it was very clean and neat. Krysta's room was decorated like a princess. Chike's room was beige, black and white. His king size bed was covered in an African design comforter set.

After taking a very long, hot shower, my stomach started growling. I hadn't eaten anything all day so I went to the kitchen to see what I could find to eat. The refrigerator was loaded with food, so I decided to cook something quick. I was sure Khalil wouldn't be calling until night fall, so I had a few hours to spare.

About an hour later, Chike came back with my bag. I was sitting at the dining room table eating fried chicken wings and sweet potato fries.

"You want some?" I asked smiling at him as I munched on my chicken.

"How da hell you gon' offer me my food in my house?" he asked staring down at me.

"Boy, sit down and eat before I eat it all," I said putting another piece of chicken on my plate.

"Fat ass," he said before I started fixing his plate.

He discussed the plan for saving Quay with me as we ate. I wanted to ask him about his plans with Quay, but I felt like it wasn't my place. My curiosity about them wasn't for her. I wanted to know how he felt about her.

"Stop checking the phone. He'll call. I'm going to take a shower," he said standing up. He must have noticed that I kept checking my phone to make sure I didn't miss Khalil's call.

After I was done cleaning the kitchen, I went into the den. My favorite part of *Love Jones* was on when Nina walked in the house taking control of Darius. I think at that moment she realized her feelings were deep for him. Thirty minutes later, Chike walked into the den with nothing but a pair of grey sweats on.

"Damn mosquitos ate yo ass up," he said staring at my thighs as he flopped down on the sofa beside me. The way his eyes ogled me spoke to my pussy. I held my thighs together trying to fight the thumping feeling he was giving me.

"You think he's going to call? You think he's hurt Quay?" I asked.

"Stop asking me them dumb ass questions. I ain't in his damn head, and I ain't there to see what da fuck going on," he said angrily.

I jumped off the sofa. "You don't even care if she's okay. I can do this on my own."

I tried to walk past him, but he grabbed the hem of my shirt. I jerked away from him only for him to grab his boxers that I wore. When his strong, masculine hand pulled me closer to him by my thigh, my body shivered. I stood in front of him unable to move as he stared at his hand on my thigh. His hands slowly started caressing my thighs causing my wetness to spill between my thighs.

He looked up at me as his hands moved to the waist of the boxers. My eyes spoke what my mouth wouldn't. I wanted what I swore I would never do again. He slid the boxers down my thighs before they dropped to my ankles. His hand stroked over my mound. He leaned forward and stroked his tongue along my inner thighs. My legs trembled and he gripped my thighs spreading my legs apart. I shut my eyes tight and whimpered when I felt his wet, warm, tongue stroking against my lower lips. He moaned when his tongue slipped between my lips.

"Aaaaahhh," I moaned softly digging my nails into his shoulders. He licked and slurped between my folds until my juices were sliding down my thighs. His tongue twirled and glided as he slurped my wet pussy.

"Gggrrr," he growled wrapping his arms around my thighs. He picked me up and leaned his head back on the black, leather sofa. He gripped my ass cheeks with his face buried deep between my thighs and devoured me. My moans and cries of ecstasy sang along with the sounds of slurping and smacking. My hips gyrated as I feed him what he desired. He flicked his tongue over my swollen clit and my hips started twirling uncontrollably.

"Fuuucckkk!" I yelped feeling my soul getting ready to be snatched from me. I tried getting away from him, but he locked me down by my thighs. He was groaning and grunting as he allowed my juices to saturate his face.

"I'm bout to come!" I screamed trying to warn him before he drowned in my essence. Hearing those words turned him into a savage. He licked, sucked and slurped my pussy with no mercy. The sounds coming from him was like a man eating a meal after days of starvation. The moment he sucked my thudding clit into his mouth, I came.

"Ooooohhhh! Ssssshhhit! Chhhhhike!" I screamed as my body froze and trembled.

My essence gushed from my body splashing against his face. I came so hard I could hear bells ringing in my head. He was growling like a famished animal as he feasted on my essence. I squealed when he flipped me over on the couch. He spread my legs, pushed them over my head and continued to satisfy his hunger. He didn't stop until I christened him again. When he finally stopped, all I could do was lie there with tears running down the sides of my face.

They should've been tears of guilt, but they were full of complete bliss. He sat up wiping the essence that dripped from his goatee with the back of his hand. My low eyes glanced at his dark chocolate face glistening from my juices. I watched him grab his phone as if he didn't just snatch my soul. He didn't even look at me when I sat up. I sat there beside him quietly not knowing what to say.

"Don't start with the guilt shit. Just come ride this dick," he said and finally looked at me. I did just that. I straddled his lap and pulled his rock-hard dick from his sweats. He groaned as he slid inside my wetness. His lips were calling mine. Kissing is personal, but I couldn't resist. I leaned forward and stroked my tongue over his bottom lip. When he tried to kiss me, I pulled my head away. I could feel his mushroom head tapping against my spot as I gyrated my hips. Wrapping his arms around my waist, I rested my forehead against his. When our lips touched each other, he sucked my swollen bottom lip into his mouth. Goosebumps covered my body as my tongue slid inside his mouth. Our tongues danced together as I rode him with heavy breathing and saliva sharing. We didn't break our kiss until we exploded together. After the numbness left my legs, I stood up to go clean myself up.

I jumped when I heard my phone rang.

Chike

"I'm so scared," Crue said as we drove toward the meeting spot. This nigga was as simple as they came. I knew he would pick a deserted location like a warehouse.

"Just don't panic. I'll be there. When he asks for the bag, just throw it at him. When he bends down to open the bag, scream to Quay to run. Just get the fuck out of the way. I'll take it from there." She nodded her head. I stopped her car about a half a mile from the warehouse and pulled over to the side of the road.

"Sit here for about five minutes. Give me time to get there," I instructed her. She looked at me with so much fear in her eyes.

"I told you I gotchu," I promised her. She forced a smile and nodded her head. I got out the car and headed toward the woods that would lead me to the warehouse. I stopped when I heard Crue calling my name. I turned to see her rushing up to me.

"What's wrong?" I asked. She got on her tiptoes and gave me the softest, wet kiss that made my dick hard and heart pound.

"I'll never get to do that again," she said with sad eyes. This wasn't the time to discuss our situation, but there was no way that was the end of whatever was going on between us. She ran back and got in the car.

*****

I had the perfect view of Khalil. His dumb ass was pacing back and forth in the middle of the empty warehouse. I could've taken him out right then, but I didn't see Quay. I needed to know she was there before I killed him. I sat patiently until the warehouse door open. Crue walked, slowly, into the warehouse. I aimed my gun at Khalil praying he didn't reach for his to kill Crue.

"Bitch, you better not be a dollar short," he said as she moved closer toward him.

She looked around. "Where's Quay. You promised me you would let her go if I gave you the money."

"That bitch here. Let me get my money first. Then you can have the bitch," he said.

"No! I need to know she's okay," Crue said.

He laughed. "I can kill yo stupid ass right now and take the money if I want. I don't have to prove shit to you."

"Please Khalil. Kill me if you're that mad about your money, but please let her go. She didn't even want to rob you. I talked her into doing it with me," she pleaded. Damn, she was a loyal ass friend.

"Shut da fuck up with them fake ass tears. Quay bring yo hoe ass out," he demanded in a loud voice. Quay slowly walked from behind a stack of crates; her eyes were bloodshot red from crying. I felt bad for her when I saw how scared she looked. Something didn't seem right about Khalil leaving her behind the crates alone. *Why would he leave her standing behind the crates instead of with him?* I glanced at the stack of crates, and my heart skipped a beat. He wasn't alone. I slowly moved to get a better view of who was with him.

"Now, throw me my money," he said with Quay standing beside him. My plan had changed. I just hoped the distraction would be enough for them to get away from Khalil. I needed to take the nigga out who was standing behind the crates. The gunshots should distract him along with the surprise in the bag.

"Now, throw me the bag before I kill this bitch," he ordered Crue again. When Crue threw the bag at his feet, she called out for Quay to come to her. Like I suspected he would do, Khalil gave the bag his undivided attention. He kneeled to open the bag. I aimed my gun at the target behind the crate.

"Fuck!" Khalil barked when the dye blew up in his face.

I let off rounds taking out the target behind the crates. His body fell knocking over the crates. I turn to take out Khalil, but he had pulled out his gun. We started firing shots at each other, and I lost him when he moved behind another stack of crates. I moved closer with my gun aimed. He let off more shots, making a run for the back door. My gun fired back. He screamed out in pain but kept running. I chased after him, but he had already hopped in his car and sped off. One of us would have to die. Which meant I'd have to find him before he found me. I had been in the game long enough to know, you never let a nigga live that tried to kill you. They always came back.

"Chike!" Quay called my name. I walked back into the warehouse. She rushed to me and threw her arms around me kissing me all over my face as she cried uncontrollably. I looked over Quay's shoulder to see Crue dropped her head. This was more of a fucked-up situation for her than me.

*****

I drove Crue's car while she sat in the backseat with Quay. Quay cried herself to sleep. I kept glancing at Crue through the rearview mirror, but she would never look at me. Stress and a mixture of confused emotion was written on her face. I never meant for things to happen between me and Crue, but they did. I didn't know what would become of us, but I did know things between me, and Quay were over. I didn't play with a woman's heart. I couldn't fake having feelings for her just because she had them for me. I liked her, but not in the way she was feeling me. I had always been upfront with her. My only regret was not ending things when I knew she had caught feelings. Crue woke Quay up when I pulled into my driveway.

"Where are we?" Quay asked looking around. For the first time since we left the warehouse, Crue looked at me through the rearview mirror. She wanted an explanation as to why Quay didn't know this was my house. It was because I never had her at my place. We always hit up hotels. This had always been my sanctuary. Only those close to me knew about my home. Most people thought I lived with my mom.

"My spot," I said getting out the car. As we were getting out the car, Quan pulled up behind my car.

"Damn nigga, I been blowing yo phone up. Where da fuck you been?" He said getting out his car. He stopped in his tracks when he spotted Crue getting out the backseat.

"What da fuck you doing with this trifling ass bitch?" he asked angrily.

"Nigga fuck you! I did some dumb shit. You ain't lose shit! Get over it. I'm the only one that lost something," Crue said getting in his face.

A scowl covered his face. "Bitch, what you lose?"

"My mothafuckin' time fuckin' yo weak dick ass," she said with venom. Her mouth was one of her biggest problems. Some shit you didn't say to a nigga. I reacted quickly when I saw Quan's hand go up in the air. He was ready to slap the shit out of her, but I jumped in front of her.

"Damn, you taking up for this bitch again. Yo Quay, she might be fuckin' yo nigga here. You know she'll do it," he said to Quay looking over my shoulder. My fist landed against his jaw. He stumbled backwards but caught himself before he fell. He charged me and we tied up on the ground. I wasn't trying to fight him. Quan was like my brother. I understood why he was mad at Crue, but it wasn't like he gave a damn if she was fucking me. He was only using Crue for sex like most of the females he fucked with. It made me mad that she didn't see that. Crue and Quay were yelling for us to stop. We didn't stop until I got him in a position where he couldn't move. After he calmed down, I let him go.

"Weak ass can't fight or fuck!" Crue said laughing. I had heard enough of her mouth. It reminded me of why I didn't like her when we first met. I turned around and faced her.

"Shut da fuck up with yo dumb ass. You fucked him for pennies, so what that make you?" I said furiously. Her mouth slightly opened, and her eyes were full of shock. I didn't mean to say it, but she pissed me off with her mouth.

"Y'all stop it please!" Quay cried out. Crue hugged her as she started to cry again.

"Take her in the damn house," I told Crue.

I turned to face Quan holding out my hand for him to shake. He stared at me for a few seconds before shaking my hand. Without giving him too many details, I told him why Crue was trying to rob him. He didn't like it, but he understood. He knew we would've done the same for each other if it was one of us. Even though he didn't care about Crue on that level, I wasn't going to tell him what happened between us. That made me realize how hard it would be for Crue to tell Quay.

"On some real shit, I ain't dumb, nigga. We been in this shit from the dirt together. Ain't but two things that make us beef and that's love for a female or money. We making money together, so that ain't the problem. I ain't the one in love, so are you?" he asked glaring me down.

"Yea, I'm in love with making money," I said trying to hide my guilt. I wasn't in love with Crue, but I felt something. I just didn't know what it was.

Quan laughed. "I got a front row seat for this show. I can't wait to see how this turns out."

Without me telling him, Quan knew what was going on. That was just how well we knew each other. Men were different from women. There was no way Quay would take what happened between me and Crue like Quan did. And just like that, we started talking about the shipment that was coming in tonight. I was exhausted. The sun had come up, and all I wanted to do was sleep. After Quan left, I went back in the house. When I walked in the house, Crue was pacing the floor.

"You need to watch yo got damn mouth," I said angrily to her.

"You don't have to worry about hearing my mouth again. As soon as Quay showers, we leaving," she said.

"No, I want to stay here with Chike," Quay said coming out the bathroom. She walked over and stood beside me.

"I'm not staying here with this disrespectful ass nigga. Come on, let's go, Quay" Crue said rolling her eyes at me and walking out the house.

"Please tell her I can stay here. What if Khalil comes looking for us?" Quay said looking terrified. I rushed out the door to stop Crue. There was a chance that Khalil could come after her again.

"Yo, that nigga still out there. Where da fuck you going?" I asked as she got in the car.

"I'll be fine. Quay needs you now. She's a mess. Tell her to call me later. I'm going to stay with Vanity and Echon until I figure something out," she said with water in her eyes.

"Get out the car, Crue," I said as she closed the door.

"I can't. You know this is wrong. I've hurt her enough. She can offer you more than just sex," she said starting her car. I tried to open her door, but she locked it. I watched her until she left the driveway.

Jedrek

Zelda sat up in her bed holding our son. This was the picture of my happiness, and I was ready to give up everything for them. I had made enough money to give them and Drekia the life I wanted them to have. The only thing missing from this picture was Drekia. I was just waiting on a call from Aunt Dee to let me know the surgery was a success. Until then, I was going to enjoy the picture in front of me.

"Come and sit down beside me," Zelda said smiling. She was doing much better, and I wanted her home, but this was the best place for her until she was well.

"You know I'm gon' fuck you until you cry when you get out of here," I said seriously.

"If I don't make you cry first," she said winking her eye. I laughed.

"Look in that drawer and get those papers out," she told me. I reached in the nightstand and got the papers. Without looking at them, I placed them on her lap.

"I know you ain't trying to work in here," I said trying to get mad at her.

"No, I'm not; those are for you," she said. I took the papers from her lap, stood up and started scanning through them. I didn't understand why she felt the need to have these papers drawn up. She survived the gunshot. Now, she was in the healing process. The papers were a copy of her revised and updated will. Since we weren't married when Lil J was born, he hadn't been legitimatized. The papers gave me custody of our son in the unimaginable event of her death.

"What you doing this for?" I asked staring at her.

"Sign them first please," she said.

Zelda was a lawyer, so she always believed in settling situations before they became complicated. I guess with her near-death experience she wanted to make sure Lil J would always be mine. I didn't need paperwork for that. Death would come to anyone that tried to take him from me. I grabbed a pen from the nightstand and signed them. There were other parts of the will discussing her finances but none of that mattered to me. Only our son was my concern. I sat back down in the chair.

"Now, what's up?" I asked.

"My heart rate isn't improving because of damaged arteries. I'm having surgery in a couple of days to correct the damage. I just need to know you and Lil J will have each other if something goes wrong," she said with tears in her eyes. There was that fear again creeping up on me, but I couldn't let her see it. She didn't need to see me scared of losing her. I needed her to see that I knew she was going to be just fine. I took the papers from the nightstand and tore them up.

"Ain't shit gon' happen to you. Who's the doctor doing the surgery?" I asked.

"I don't want you to know. All you are going to do is threaten to kill him if something goes wrong. I need him calm and steady while fucking with my heart," she said seriously.

"I ain't letting no-got-damn-body cut on you without knowing who it is," I said, and I jumped up.

"It's not your call. It's my decision. My parents and Vanity have met and talked with him," she informed me.

I flopped back down in the chair. "You serious right now?"

"Yes, I've prayed about this, and I know God will be with me. I need you to have that same faith with me," she said reaching over and holding my hand.

"He better or I'm gon' fuck His ass up," I said.

She laughed. "And what exactly are you going to do to God?"

"Not a damn thang, because you gon' come through this shit," I said staring at her. She filled me in about her surgery. I hated that I didn't know the doctor, but she was right. I probably would hold his family at gun point until she came out the surgery like I did Drekia's doctor. I didn't have them at gun point, but he knew they would die if Drekia didn't survive. The universe didn't bring her into my life to take her away. We had a lifetime to spend together.

"You think if I fucked you in this bed, it'll speed up your heart rate?" I asked with a smile.

She laughed. "It'll probably kill me."

Two Days Later

Everyone sat in the family waiting area waiting for Zelda to get out of surgery. I tried to stay as calm as I could, but I was losing patience. A nurse came and gave us an update that everything was going well, but I needed it to be over. I needed to know she was going to be okay. After a couple more hours a short, stocky, dark complexioned man came into the room. He removed his mask and revealed a big smile.

"Everything went well. She'll be out for a while. Once we move her into a recovery room, you can start visiting two at a time," he said looking around the room.

My entire body relaxed. He went into more details about the surgery, but I didn't care about any of that. All I needed to know was that she was going to be okay. The remainder of our day was spent at the hospital with Zelda. She was in and out of consciousness for most of our visit. It was hospital policy that no one could stay overnight in the recovery unit, but I broke policy. I slept by her bed in a small chair that entire night. She was still asleep when I left. I wanted to go home, shower, check on Lil J and come back to be with her. As I was driving home, Aunt Dee called my phone.

"God is good. She's awake and remembers everything," Aunt Dee said with a soft cry. I couldn't stop the big smile that spread across my face. Drekia's surgery was four days ago, but she had been sleeping in and out of consciousness. When she was awake, it was only for a short time and wasn't speaking and aware of her surroundings. Sometimes she wasn't aware of who she was. Dr. Abei said it was normal after going through the surgery. We still couldn't help from worrying about her.

"Where she at? Put her on the phone."

Aunt Dee laughed. "Slow down. Dr. Abei is examining her. I just stepped out to call you. We don't know if the surgery worked or not. He said there are several tests he needs to run."

"I don't give a damn about that. I just want her alive and home," I said.

"I know. I'll call you back as soon as the doctor is done talking to her," she said.

"A'ight. Thanks for being there for her, Aunt Dee," I said gratefully.

"Oh boy please. I'm in Switzerland living my best life," she said laughing. I laughed with her.

"Oh yea, Vonna left early this morning. She needed to get back home," she said.

"That's why I needed you there. I knew she wouldn't stick it out with Drekia," I said shaking my head.

"You aren't on a killing spree, so I take it Zelda's surgery went well?" she asked.

"She's good. I just left the hospital to go home and shower," I told her. I glanced through my rearview mirror to see the same car following me from when I left the hospital.

"Let me call you back, Aunt Dee," I said not waiting for a reply.

I made a couple of turns to see if the car would follow me, but it didn't. I guess I was paranoid since I still had no idea who did this to Zelda. Now, that I knew she was okay, it was time to put in work and find who did it. I was sitting at the stop light when a black Benz pulled up and rolled down the window. A nine-millimeter appeared, and shots started hitting my passenger window. The bullet pierced through the window and hit the driver's side window; shattering the glass. I grabbed my gun from under the seat and jumped out the car. Ducking behind the car, I fired back at the vehicle until the car sped off leaving nothing but smoke.

I looked around to see people scattering for cover while others looked to see what was going on. I hurried and jumped in my car and left. I drove straight to Chike's house. We had to find whoever this was trying to take me out. I knew it was the same people that shot Zelda. I was surprised to see Crue's car parked in the driveway, but Chike's car wasn't there. I noticed the front door open when I got out the car. I quickly made my way inside thinking whoever shot at me came at Chike. All I heard was Quay and Crue bickering. I made my way toward the den following their voices.

"I told you I don't' like being at his house. Let's go. I'm hungry," Crue said.

"I don't know why you don't like him. He saved my life and yours from Jedrek. Khalil would've killed me, and Jedrek would've killed you if he knew what really happened to Zelda," Quay said.

"Shut up! I don't want to think about that. It's over. Just get your purse and let's go," Crue said anxiously.

"What up, Drek?" Chike said from behind me walking in his front door. I ignored him and walked into the den shocking Crue and Quay. They looked like they were staring death in his face. If what they said was true, they were right.

"I-I'm sorry, Jedrek. I didn't mean for none of this to happen," Crue said backing away from me. Chike came from behind me and stood in front of Crue.

I stared at him with heated blood running through my veins. "You knew about this?"

"Yea," he replied honestly. Crue stood behind him with fear in her eyes. She knew she was facing death.

"I'll kill all three of y'all right now. I'm giving you a chance to live, nigga. Move," I demanded of him.

"Please don't kill him! He was only trying to save our lives," Quay pleaded with me.

"I know this fucked up, but I did what I had to do. Killing us ain't gon' solve shit. You always taught me not to move on emotions. That's why I didn't come to you with this. I know you would've handled it with your emotions because it was Zelda. Think about what this will do to her if she loses her family," Chike said calmly. He didn't blink. I wouldn't expect any less from him. He was my protégé. My heart didn't want to admit it, but my mind knew he was right. I looked over his shoulder at Crue.

"If I lay eyes on you again, I will kill you," I told her. She took a few more steps back.

I gave Chike my attention. "You got an hour to be at my house or yo ass is dead with her." I walked out before I killed all of them.

Quay

I love Crue, but after watching Chike defend her, I wanted her dead as much as Jedrek wanted to kill her. He was willing to lose his own life for her. Everything he had done was about saving her. Nothing was done because of his feelings for me. The couple of days I had been at his house, he had hardly here. He never asked me how I was doing after being kidnapped or anything. If I couldn't make him stop falling for her, I'd have to make her walk away from him. I could smell him on her and knowing they had been intimate sickened me. I was not giving up on him but first I must get her out of the way.

"Go to Ma's house," Chike said turning around to face Crue.

"No, I have enough people involved in my mess," she said walking out the den.

"Go meet Drek. I'll go with her to make sure she's okay," I said. I took my chances, tiptoed and kissed him softly on the lips. I smiled when he didn't reject me. Before we could pull out the driveway, Chike came jogging toward the car. He held out a black card.

"Get a room until I smooth shit over with Jedrek," he said to Crue. He had never given me money. I didn't understand why she was so special to be given money. She was the reason we were in this mess.

"Thank you, but I can't take that," she said softly to him.

"I didn't say have it. I'll get it back. Don't use my shit for shopping sprees. Pay for the room and food. That's it," he said sternly.

"I really appreciate this. I promise I'll find a way to pay you back," she said looking at him.

"Make sure it ain't the old-fashioned way," he said before walking off. He knew she was a hoe. There was no way he would try to build a relationship with her. I didn't know why I was stressing over them fucking. He may have fucked her, but he was going to love me.

We drove around until Crue pulled up to and Embassy Suite. After checking into a room, we started talking about Jedrek and if he would kill us. I knew he wasn't going to kill me. I was a victim like him and Zelda. She was the only one on his death wish. Even though she fucked Chike, I didn't want her dead. She was still my best friend. I just wanted my happiness for once. I was always doing things to benefit her. It was time for me to do things for myself.

"I have to eat when I'm stressing. I'm going to order room service," Crue said.

"No, I'm sure he didn't mean run up his card on room service. Let's just go out and get something to eat," I suggested. I didn't want her wasting his money like it was hers. If I couldn't waste it, she couldn't either.

"You think he can calm Jedrek down?" she asked worriedly.

"I hope so. He was furious, but he respects Chike. He was so sexy standing up to Jedrek. That's gone be my husband one day. I can feel it," I said. She dropped her head.

"I haven't really had a chance to tell you how sorry I am for getting you in this mess. I should've told you Khalil was here. After the run in I had with him at the clinic, I thought he had left. I still don't understand how he knew I was there," she explained. It was time to put on the water works.

"I was so scared, Crue. He wanted to kill me, but I begged him for my life. I was the one that gave him the code to Zelda's house, but she wasn't supposed to be there. Her jewelry was enough to settle our debt to him. He became furious when things went bad. That's when he called you and demanded the money or he was going to kill me. I'm so sorry for putting Zelda's life at risk. I swear I didn't want that to happen to her," I said crying my eyes out. I honestly was sorry for what happened to Zelda. Crue wrapped her arms around me.

"None of this is your fault. I begged you to rob him with me. He wanted to do a threesome, so I needed you there to get in his bedroom. I know you would never hurt Zelda. You were only trying to save your life," she said. I started to cry harder.

"He beat and raped me, Crue." She started crying with me. We cried together as she promised to be there and help me through my ordeal.

"I know you don't like him, but can you help me win Chike over? You know how to play on a man's heart. I don't have that skill. He's been so distant with me, and I don't know what I'm doing wrong. He has to like me enough that he was willing to risk his life," I said playing on her emotions. She sat quietly before she responded.

"Yea, I'll make sure you have your chance with him," she said.

A Day Later

I was in Chike's kitchen cooking him a home cooked meal when he walked in the house. I stayed a couple of hours with Crue pouring my heart out about the kidnapping and Chike. Her guilt was eating her alive. Bypassing the kitchen, he went straight to his bedroom. I followed him to his bedroom to see him removing his shirt. He wasn't flashy nor did he wear expensive designer clothes. His sex appeal was effortless. I walked and stood in front of him.

"I cooked dinner for us," I said massaging his chest and abs. His aroma of sweat and cologne excited me.

"I'm good. Why da fuck that nigga coming for Jedrek?" he asked.

"He wasn't coming for Jedrek at first. His concern was his money until he shot Zelda. I tried to scare them by letting them know Jedrek was coming for them. Khalil remembered Jedrek's name, and that Jedrek killed Khalil's uncle. He wants revenge."

"Why da fuck you ain't tell me this sooner?" he asked angrily.

"I'm still trying to get over everything Khalil put me through. I haven't been thinking clearly. I'm still scared for my life, Chike," I said with crocodile tears.

"I gotta go back out," he said putting his shirt back on. I grabbed him by his hand before he walked out the bedroom.

"I'm sorry I didn't tell you about the things Crue made me do. I know she was wrong for playing and sleeping with different men for money, but she's my best friend. I can't judge her. So many times, I wanted to tell her no, but she would make me feel bad if I didn't help her," I explained to him. I needed it to sound like Crue was the worst kind of woman. Crue didn't sleep with a lot of the men she robbed. She only slept with a couple of the guys that caked her with expensive shit.

"You a grown ass woman and can't let someone dictate your life," he said.

"I'm trying to have a better life here. Things were bad for me back home. This was supposed to be a fresh start for us. You've been a great friend to me since I've been here. You are one of the reasons that I want to make my life better. Please don't let my past mistakes ruin our friendship," I said gazing up at him.

"A platonic friendship is all I can offer you," he said.

"Is it someone else?" I asked. It would crush my heart if he said yes. My eyes filled up with tears hoping he didn't tell me he wanted someone else. I knew in my heart that someone else would be Crue.

"Nah," he said bluntly before walking out the room.

Six Weeks Later

Zelda

My heart was full. My surgery went well and now I was at home relaxing. Work and my goals were my only focus at one time. Now, I have a handsome son and a man that got all my attention. Making sure my family was happy and loved came before anything. I still wanted my career as a successful lawyer, but my priorities had changed. I was doing so well after my surgery; I was released earlier than expected, and it felt good being home. Clyde followed me everywhere I went in the house. He would sleep by our bed every night. Nights when Jedrek wouldn't let him in the room, he slept outside the bedroom door. I watched Jedrek as he dressed. I had seen that look in his eyes before.

"Where you going?" I asked climbing out of bed.

"Handle some business," he replied without looking at me. I walked over and made him look me in the eyes.

"Do whatever you need to do to protect our family," I said. I knew whatever business he was going to handle was related to my shooting.

"The nurse is here if you need anything," he said not acknowledging my statement. I didn't need a reply. I knew what he was capable of doing.

"It's time for me to get back to work, so I'm going to crack open my dusty laptop," I said smiling.

"Don't forget about my damn son sleeping in the next room," he said seriously.

I laughed. "Boy hush, he'll wake his greedy behind up screaming like he's starving."

"I know that feeling," he said staring at me with lustful eyes. I giggled. We hadn't had sex in two months. The doctor recommended no sexual activity for sex weeks and I obliged because Jedrek's sex game would send me back in the hospital.

"I talked with Drekia this morning. She's doing great. She's started to remember more, but still has a lot of time gaps," I told him. Drekia's surgery looked to be a success. She had been going through several brain activity tests and the damage seemed to have been repaired.

"She says she wants a convertible Benz parked in the driveway when she gets home," he said smiling. It wasn't often that he showed his pearly whites. Seeing him smiling and happy filled my heart with joy.

I laughed. "We gotta teach her how to drive all over again before we make that happen."

He stopped smiling and caressed the side of my face with his strong hand. His eyes gazed over my face as he licked his lips. My heart fluttered and pussy jumped. I was too familiar with the look in his eyes. His lips softly pressed against mine. I released a soft moan when his wet tongue slid inside my mouth. This was the moment my body had been craving. My six-week checkup wasn't until tomorrow, but my body wanted what it wanted. I was willing to risk my life for the feelings he gave me. His hand slid between my thighs at the same moment that Lil J's cries came through the baby monitor.

"Damn," Jedrek said breaking our kiss. I laughed. I hurried to get our greedy boy as he left to handle business.

An hour later, I was sitting in the baby's room enjoying time with Lil J when my cellphone rang. I had only spoken to Crue over the phone. She hadn't been to see me or Lil J since my surgery. Something was going on with her, but I couldn't get her to talk to me. It was time for me to be the role model I was supposed to be for her.

"Hey niece," I said jokingly answering the phone.

She laughed. "Hey Auntie, how's my lil cousin?"

"Greedy, come over and spend some time with us," I suggested.

"I wish I could but I'm at work. Maybe some other time," she said sadly.

She told me she was working at a hotel as a desk clerk. If she wasn't willing to come to me, I'd go to her. I just had to make sure I was back home before Jedrek got here. He would have a fit if he knew I left the house. I played with Lil J until he fell asleep. After taking a shower and getting dressed, I told the nurse I'd be leaving for a while.

*****

"How may I help you?" The lady at the front desk asked. The middle-aged black woman's badge read manager.

"Hi, I'm looking for an employee by the name of Cruella. She's a desk clerk here. She told me she was at work. Maybe I have the wrong Drury Inn," I said looking around.

"No sweetie, you have the right one. She's not a desk clerk though. She's a housekeeper," she said.

My mouth dropped open. I would never imagine Crue taking a job as a maid. There was nothing wrong with the job. It was just something Crue felt was beneath the life she wanted to live. Now, I know there was something going on with her.

"Is she here today?" I asked. The woman looked at a clipboard before informing me Crue was working on the fifth floor.

"Thank you," I said before making my way to the elevator. When I reached the fifth floor, I saw the housekeeper's cart. I didn't know which room she was in, so I stood by the cart waiting for her to come out. When she stepped outside of room 514, she dropped the bottle of cleaning fluids from her hand.

"Look at you working hard for the paper," I said smiling at her. She rolled her eyes before reaching down to pick up the bottle.

"What are you doing here?" she asked angrily.

"I came to talk to you. You've been acting distant and I want to know why. We're family and I love you. What's going on with you?" I asked. Her eyes started to fill with tears. I took her by the hand and walked back into the room with her. We sat down on the bed and she wiped her tears before they fell.

"I'm not here to judge you, Crue. You are young. This is the time to make mistakes. I just want you to know I'm here for you," I promised her.

She looked at me with remorse and regret in her eyes. "I'm the reason you got shot. I robbed a guy for fifty-grand. That money burned in my old car. He kidnapped Quay so I told him to rob your house to get the money I owed him. I didn't know he was going to do it the day you were there. I'm so sorry for what I did."

I was hurt and angry with her, but I could see how sorry she was. I couldn't let her mistake stop her from having the life she wanted. She needed people in her life that showed support and love for her. Me walking away from her would only cause her to continue making bad choices. I held her until she stopped crying, then she filled me in on everything that happened. I now knew who Jedrek was seeking to kill.

"How's Quay doing?" I asked.

"She's doing much better. Chike is helping her get over what I caused," she said dropping her head.

I lifted her chin turning her head to look at me. "You chose your friendship over your feelings for him."

She wiped her tears and stood up. "It wasn't hard. We had a sexual attraction. It's over."

She could lie to me, but she couldn't lie to herself. I could see it in her eyes; her feelings for Chike weren't only sexual. Guilt was making her choose to walk away from him. Some things I must let her decide on her own, and this was one of them. My goal was to give her the support to make better choices in her life.

"Where are you staying?" I asked.

"Here. The manager is really nice. She lets me stay here and gave me a job. The job sucks but it comes with a roof over my head," she said.

"Well, keep the job. It builds character. When you get off today, come home to Jedrek's house. Don't worry about him, he's not going to kill you," I said smiling at her.

"No Zelda. I don't blame him for wanting to kill me. I almost caused him and Lil J to lose you. I'm not coming there to ruin his happiness by him having to look at me. I'm fine here. I promise," she explained.

I shrugged my shoulders. "Fine, but know you are always welcome. So, what's your game plan?"

She flopped down on the side of the bed. "To survive. Everyone isn't meant to live the life they want. I think I'm one of those people."

"Oh hell no. You are meant to live the life you fight for. People battle shit every day and still fight hard for what they want in life. I'll give you three days to sulk in your own misery. After those three days, we will sit down and talk about what it is that Cruella wants out of life. Matter of fact, when I come back here, I want you to have a plan laid out on paper of the goals you want to achieve," I informed her.

She smiled and hugged me tight. "Thank you for forgiving me."

*****

My heart dropped when I saw Jedrek's car. I never expected him to come home this quick. I reached for my phone and saw numerous missed calls from him and Vanity. My phone stayed on silent when I was enjoying time with Lil J. I forgot to turn the volume up when I left to visit Crue. My poor little heart was beating rapidly as I made my way in the house. The nurse gave me a cautious look when I passed the kitchen letting me know Jedrek was furious.

He was changing Lil J's pamper when I walked into the nursery. We didn't say anything to each other. I went to our bedroom to wait for his wrath. Sleep came down on me while I waited to get the argue over.

When I woke up, the room was pitch black. I made my way to Lil J's room to see him asleep in his crib. I searched the house until I found Jedrek in the sauna. He always came in here after a workout. Most of his workouts were done to relieve anger and stress. He stared at me with cold eyes. Sweat dripped from his chocolate body making me forget he was furious with me. I pulled his T-shirt that covered my naked body over my head. His eyelids closed trying to fight the temptation I was giving him. I walked over and straddled his lap.

"I know you are mad, and you have every right to be, but right now I want what we both crave," I whispered in his ear while licking and biting his earlobe. I could feel his erection growing against my mound. I held his face between my hands and covered his mouth with mine. He groaned inside my mouth as he sucked my tongue into his. His hand massaged my thighs as he kissed and licked my moist skin. My body shivered when his fingers slipped between my wet fold.

"Aaaahhh yeesss," I moaned softly as he licked and sucked on my breasts. His teeth sunk into my hard nipples. My hips twirled feeling the friction of his bulge under his towel rub against my clit. I reached down and unwrapped the towel to free his brick hard dick., I slid down on his throbbing shaft.

"Ssssshhhit," he barked under his breath gripping my ass cheeks. My pussy walls caved in around his shaft as I gyrated and bucked my hips. My wetness coated him spilling out of my tunnel and onto the base of his dick. His hands ran up and down my back as his kissed and caressed my neck, shoulders and breasts with his tongue. He rammed his dick deeper inside of me violating my spot. My head fell back as I exploded in ecstasy.

"Ooooohhh yeeeeesss!" I screamed as my essence flowed freely onto him.

"Fuck! Yo heart," he barked stopping in the middle of giving me exactly what I'd been starving for. I leaned forward wrapping my arms around his neck and whispering pleads for more.

"Keep fucking me. I want all of it. Please don't stop," I begged rocking my hips. Squishy sounds of my essence smacking against our bodies echoed through the room. He stood up, cuffing my legs in his arms and placing me against the wall.

"Damn, you feel so mothafuckin' good," he groaned drilling inside me. My nails dug into his back as my juices slid down my inner thighs. My loud screams of pleasure shouted out as he brought me to another orgasm. He grunted and growled as he kept driving inside my trenched wetness. My nails scraped across his back and I clung on to my sanity. His way of fucking me was driving me insane. My walls tightened around his shaft bracing for my body to release again.

"Come on this dick!" he demanded. He slipped two of his fingers into my ass and I let go with a force. My pussy gushed as cream oozed all over him.

"Aaaarrrrgghhhh! Fuuuccckkk!" His body jerked like a thousand volts of electricity hit him. I collapsed in his arms resting my head on his shoulder.

Crue

"I'm so happy to see you. How have you been?" Quay asked, hugging me. We were sitting in my cramped little room relaxing. I had been so scared Jedrek was coming to kill me. Quay told me about Khalil connection to Jedrek, and that gave Jedrek more reason to want me dead.

Sometimes I hated when Quay come over, because the only thing she wanted to talk about was Chike. I demanded she didn't tell him where I was staying, and she had kept her promise so far. With everything I put Quay through, she deserved her chance with Chike. I didn't know if I could fight temptation if I was to be around him.

"I've been good. Just working. You are looking great," I said. Quaysha has gained a few pounds which was giving her the figure she always wanted. Her Peruvian body wave hair, flawless makeup and stylish clothes made her more beautiful. It filled my heart with joy to see her happy.

"No drugs. I still drink like a fish though," she said laughing. I laughed with her.

"You haven't been by in a couple of weeks. What's been going on?" I asked curiously.

"Girl, Chike's baby mama is the one to thank for me leaving drugs alone. That bitch strung out bad. She be coming by our house begging for money and drugs. She had the nerve to call the cops on him for kidnapping Krysta." The only thing ringing in my head was she said *our house.*

"How's work?" I asked not wanting to hear anything else about her and Chike.

"I'm working at the hospital and stacking my money. Chike keeps telling me I don't have to work, but I want to show him what we can accomplish together. I thought I was pregnant, but it was a false alarm. I don't know what you said to make him give me a chance, but he's been so loving and supportive of me," she said smiling at me.

I lied and told her I had a talk with Chike about her. The truth was I hadn't spoken to Chike since I left his house that day. He hadn't tried to call or find me, so I guess he got what he wanted *in* Quay and what he wanted *from* me. If he was able to get into a relationship with Quay after what happened between us, sex was all I was to him. I endured the pain of listening to her talk about Chike for a couple of hours.

After Quay left, I went to Shyma's Instagram page to see pictures of Krysta. The entire time Quay talked about Chike she never mentioned bonding with his daughter; that thought led to me missing Krysta. A smile appeared on my face when I saw her mean eyes even though she was smiling. Her hair was a mess, but she was still the cutest little girl to me.

Zelda had given me three days to waddle in my pity, but I'd decided to get my life together right then. I got dressed in a pair of distressed shorts and a spaghetti strap tank top. I put my mess of curly hair on top of my head, slipped on my Fendi slides and decided to enjoy the rest of my day.

*****

I was in Saks Fifth Avenue admiring a bomb ass pair of Red Bottoms. I looked at the price and put them down. When I turned to walk away, I bumped into a hard chest. I looked up into Gerard's eyes and quickly tried to rush past him, but he grabbed my arm.

"I ain't tripping about you killing my seed. I know it was the best decision," he said calmly.

"Well, what do you want?" I asked.

"You want them shoes?" he asked nodding toward the pair of red bottoms I so desperately wanted. I took a few seconds to debate on whether to let him buy them for me. It had been a long time since I had been on a shopping spree, and Gerard was just the nigga to give me one.

"Nah, I'm good," I said. I knew what came with him spending money on me, and I didn't want to do that anymore. My finessing ways were the reason I was in this mess. He tried to persuade me to get them, but I stated adamantly that I didn't want them.

"What you been up to?" he asked.

I shrugged my shoulders. "Nothing, just working and surviving."

"I saw Quay the other day, and she told me what happened. I ain't have shit to do with what Khalil did. He just told me you owed him some money. That shit was no concern of mine. I knew you was all about getting in a nigga's pocket. I didn't mind throwing you a few bills for the goods," he said with a smirk. I felt low as dirt and humiliated, but he was only stating facts. While I thought I was running game on niggas, they were playing me.

"I guess we both got what we wanted," I said walking away from him. Before I could make my exit, Vonna came walking up to me.

"Hey, Cruella Deville," she said calling me by the stupid ass nickname I had heard all my life.

"Hi, Vonna," I spoke dryly.

"You know my man?" She asked nodding past me at Gerard. I knew Vonna liked younger man, but Gerard was only a couple of years older than me. Gerard stood there looking like a deer caught in headlights, but he didn't have to feel ashamed or guilty; he wasn't my man. Coming from a small town, it was no surprise to find out someone you knew was fucking the same person as you.

"He's your man? He's a bit young for you, isn't he?" I asked jokingly.

"Age ain't nothing but a number. Ain't that right, baby?" she said smiling at Gerard. He didn't reply to her answer.

I laughed. "Yea, but you're twice his age. You gotta be in your fifties at least. Gerard is twenty-four."

"Let's go. I got shit to do," Gerard said trying to walk away.

"Gerard ain't no damn twenty-five. I mean he may look and fuck like he is, but he's thirty-four," she said laughing.

"What?" I asked angrily. I felt disgusted. I was fucking a suga daddy. Thirty-four wasn't old, but with me being only twenty-two years old, he was a suga daddy to me.

"You lying dog!" I yelled at Gerard.

"So, you been fucking my man and didn't know how old he was?" Vonna asked laughing at me.

"He played the role of suga daddy well," I said trying to save face.

"Yea, with another bitch's money. He don't own shit. The house, cars and money belong to a rich, old woman. He's a kept nigga," she said rolling her eyes at Gerard.

"Man, fuck both of y'all broke bitches. I told you to stay da fuck away from me until you can afford this dick," he said to Vonna.

Now it was her turn to be embarrassed. I laughed at her and walked away hearing her call his name as he hurried away in the opposite direction of me.

Moments later, chills went through my body and my heart pounded as I heard Chike calling my name. I started walking faster through the parking lot to my car.

"Crue! I know you got damn hear me. Stop before I shoot yo ass in the leg," Chike demanded furiously. When I turned to face him, he walked up to me. He wore a fitted red T-shirt, blue distressed jeans and a pair of black, red and white Givenchy sneakers. His fresh cut and trim made him look edible.

"What? What do you want?" I asked angrily. I hated that I still wanted him. My lust for him was stronger than I thought. It had been over a month since we had seen or talked to each other, but my feelings for him where stronger than ever.

"What da fuck you so mad about? Where you been?" he asked.

"Minding my business. Now, leave me alone," I said trying to walk away. He grabbed my arm and pulled me into his chest.

"Shit ain't that easy," he said staring at me. His fingertips stroked across my belly and I melted. I became drunk with my desire for him. Everything became a blur as we stared at each other. The next thing I remember was me riding his dick in the backseat of my car. Our clothes were stuck to our sweaty bodies by the time we were done.

"I can't keep doing this with you. This is so wrong," I said climbing off him.

"Ain't shit wrong about what just happened," he said stuffing his still hard dick inside his boxers.

"What just happened was I fucked the man that my best friend is in love with. That is wrong. Get out, Chike!" I said. I guess he wanted the life with Quay and sex with me.

"Yo, when I call your phone…answer," he said before opening the car door. Before he got out, he gently grabbed the back of my head pulling my head toward him. He kissed me softly on the lips before slipping me his tongue. I graciously accepted by sliding mine into his mouth. He left me dizzy in the backseat.

Chike

My body felt like it was floating when I walked in Ma's house. I had thought about Crue every day. She needed space from our involvement. When I saw her walking through the parking lot at the mall, I couldn't stay away. There was a connection between us that I couldn't resist. She was what I dreamed about when I slept.

I had been working with Jedrek trying to find Khalil, but Khalil didn't have family that we could threaten to bring him out of hiding. Genius tracked down the rental car, but it had been returned. It was one of those rental agencies that let drug traffickers rent cars with cash. Jedrek wasn't a reasonable man when it came to protecting his family. He wanted to kill everyone in the rental agency. I had to get Echon to convince him otherwise.

"Boy, what you smoking?" Ma asked when I walked in the kitchen.

"Nothing. I ain't had time to smoke," I said sitting at the table. After fixing me a plate of fried chicken, lima beans and rice, and cornbread, she sat across from me.

"What lil gal got you floating on clouds. If it ain't weed, it gotta be pussy. Pussy must've fell from heaven," she said.

"Damn Ma, I don't wanna have these kinds of conversations with you," I said sitting back in my chair.

"Well, don't come in my house smelling like sex," she said. I chuckled, shook my head and started eating.

"Is it that needy ass girl you got staying at yo house?" she asked, folding her arms.

"Nah," I answered.

"So, you still fucking the best friend," she said shaking her head.

"They ain't the only two women in Atlanta," I said not looking up at her.

"You better not be fucking Special's cracked out ass. That child needs help. I saw her walking up the road looking like death the other day," she said sadly.

"I'm trying, but she gotta want help," I told her.

"It ain't yo job to save every woman that comes into your life. Special needs your help, because she's the mother of your child. This other girl…I just don't know. You might be better off with the best friend."

I laughed. "You don't even like Crue."

"I didn't like the lil heifer until I saw her concern for my grandbaby when she thought she was hurt. Any young woman loving a child she has no connection to wins me over," she said winking her eye at me. I decided to confide in her about me and Crue. I told her Crue wanted nothing to do with me because of Quay.

"Well, you can't blame her. She's trying to be a loyal friend. You can't have one friend living with you and fucking the other one behind her back. I didn't raise you that way," she scolded me.

"It ain't even like that with me and Quay no more. She went through a lot when she was kidnapped. I'm just trying to help her through that so she can get on her feet," I explained.

"Boy, yo ass ain't no counselor. Now, I ain't 'bout to let you play with these girls' hearts. I'm a woman first. She can stay with me until she gets a place of her own," she said.

"For real?" I asked shockingly.

"Yea, I need to scope her out. Then I'll know which one is best for you," she said smiling. Krysta walked into the room rubbing her sleepy eyes. I picked her up and sat her on my lap.

"You better not kiss that baby with your mouth. Ain't no telling what you been doing with Crue," Ma said before leaving the table. Krysta jumped from my lap and ran to the front door calling Crue's name. She had been asking for her since Crue left, so when Krysta heard Ma say her name, she thought Crue was here.

I played with Krysta until my eyes wouldn't stay open. Krysta lived with me, but since Quay had been at my house, she had stayed with Ma. It was time to sit down and have a talk with Quay.

*****

Quay cooked every day, and she kept the house spotless. I told her she didn't have to do any of that, but she insisted on it. She was smart and beautiful, but I didn't feel that connection with her. Every night I would wake up to find her in my bed. She said she would get scared from the nightmares she was having. We hadn't had sex, and I didn't plan on taking it there with her again. I didn't want to give her mixed signals.

"I'm cooking fried catfish, cheese grits, coleslaw and hush puppies," she said smiling over her shoulder at me when I sat at the kitchen table.

"Come sit down for a minute," I said to her.

"Hold on. I don't want to burn this catfish. It's almost finish," she said. I sat quietly as she talked about her plan to enroll in school. I admired her for wanting to do something with her life. I had tried to force myself to feel more for her, but it just wasn't there. After she was done cooking, she brought a hefty plate and sat it in front of me. I didn't want to hurt her feelings, but I had just eaten a big plate at Ma's.

"I'm going to save this. I just ate something at Ma's house," I told her.

"Oh ok. You could've called and told me you were eating over there. I wouldn't have cooked all this food," she said disheartened.

"You're doing great things for yourself. I'm sure you are ready to move on with your life. I know you need more time to save up money, so Ma has agreed to let you move in with her until you've saved enough," I explained.

"You don't want me here?" she asked sadly.

"I just think it's best. You have feelings for me that I can't reciprocate. I don't want to hold your life up and have you thinking something will happen between us. You are beautiful and smart, Quay. Some nigga gon' be lucky to have you. Also, it's time for me to bring my daughter home. She's been staying with Ma since you've been here," I added.

"You let Crue be around your daughter, and Krysta's mother's on drugs. Why can't I stay here with you and her?" she asked.

"I don't have to explain shit about my seed to you. I'm trying to be the nigga Ma raised me to be. Accept the offer I'm giving you, or find somewhere else to go," I told her.

I didn't wait for her to reply before I walked out the kitchen. Before I could make it to my bedroom, someone was banging at my front door. I grabbed my gun from my waist. I looked at my phone screen, which allowed me to view the security camera, to see Special standing there with a battered face. I rushed and opened the door, and she collapsed in my arms. I quickly examined her to make sure there were no bullet wounds. I took her in the living room and laid her on the couch.

"Get me some wet washcloths," I told Quay. She was standing in the living room entrance staring at us in shock. She hurried away and return with what I asked. After cleaning up Special's face, her wounds weren't so bad, but she reeked of alcohol. Plus, her clothes were dingy, and she smelled bad. After bringing me the towels, Quay left me in the living room caring for Special. I ended up sleeping in the recliner that night to watch over her.

When I woke up the next morning, I found Special bent over the toilet emptying her stomach. She was once the prettiest girl I had ever seen. Now, her thick frame was skin and bones, her hair was unkempt, and her eyes were sunken into her face with dark rings around them. When we met, I was going through my rebellious stage with Ma and wanted to hang out on the street corners. Shit got so bad between me and Ma that she put me out the house. I started hustling corners for a local dealer to feed and house myself. Special copped a hit from me one night, and we started fucking with each other heavy. We fell hard for each other, and she stopped doing drugs for a while. After she had Krysta, it wasn't long before the urge was calling her again. We fought every day because I wouldn't serve her. That didn't stop her from getting her high from the next corner boy.

I leaned against the doorway staring down at her. I shook my head when I saw the bruises on her arm. She was using needles now. She swore to me she would never let her addiction get that far. I wasn't in love with her anymore, but I had love for the mother of my child. Therefore, I'd always do what I could to help her. She looked up at me looking like a zombie.

"Who beat you?" I asked. She wiped the saliva that dripped from her bottom lip with the palm of her hand.

"I don't know," she said. I had heard stories about her selling herself, so she probably didn't know who beat her.

"You gotta get some help, Special. You look like death," I told her.

She started crying. "It's too hard. That shit won't let me go. I be trying."

I walked over and kneeled in front of her. "If you wanna do this, I promise I'll be there for you. You gotta want it for yourself."

"I overslept and need a ride to work," Quay said standing in the bathroom door with her arms crossed.

"Call Uber like you been doing," I said looking over my shoulder at her.

"I'll be late for work waiting on Uber," she said agitated.

"Take my damn truck. After work, come pack yo things. You gon' be staying with Ma until you get a spot," I told her. Quay's eyes were full of jealousy. I needed to end whatever hopes she had of me and her being together.

"Fine," she said bluntly before walking away.

A Week Later

Jedrek

Drekia was finally home. Aunt Dee's family, Yella Boy and Zuri had come down just for the day to welcome her home. I had a feast catered in the dining room, and all Drekia's favorite foods were on the menu. She still didn't remember the attack. Dr. Abei said she had blocked it out and recommended counseling and therapy to help her remember. I'd let it be her decision if she wanted to remember what happened to her. The only side effects from her surgery would be severe migraines. We were all sitting around talking and laughing when Vonna decided to join us.

"There's my baby," Vonna said walking up to Drekia with her arms open. Drekia was looking at Vonna with a stare I'd never seen from her. She had always been overjoyed when Vonna came around. When Vonna hugged her, Drekia didn't return the love. I looked at Aunt Dee for an explanation of Drekia's attitude toward Vonna, but Aunt Dee shrugged her shoulders, not knowing why Drekia was acting cold toward Vonna.

"Baby, can you lay him in the bassinet," Zelda said to me. She looked tired. I knew we were fucking too much, but Zelda was like a wild animal in heat. She was fucking me every chance she got. If she wasn't feeding Lil J his bottle, she was feeding me her pussy. I wasn't complaining, because every time we fucked, it only got better.

"Go take a nap. You look tired," I told her taking Lil J from her arms.

"Yea, this has been too much excitement today," she said smiling at me. She was thinking about us having sex in the room that I was turning into her home office.

"After you wake up, eat something," I instructed. She blushed knowing what I wanted from her later. Now that Drekia was home, she could plan the wedding she wanted. We would get married right here and now if it were up to me, but she wanted a small, eloquent wedding in the backyard. She walked over and gave Drekia a hug welcoming her home again before leaving the living room.

"So, how are you? Did the surgery work?" Vonna asked Drekia. Drekia walked over to the mini-bar and poured herself a glass wine.

"Yes, but details of the day I was attacked are vague. Dr. Abei recommended therapy, but I'm not going to take it. I remember the most important details of that day," Drekia said staring at Vonna.

"Well, that's all that matters. You don't need to remember that awful day. You have a full life ahead of you now. You can start living your best life. There're so many places I want to visit with you. We're going to travel the world together," Vonna said cheerfully.

Drekia took a step back from Vonna. "No, I will be traveling by myself or with the people that were there for me when I needed *you* the most."

Tears started welling up in Drekia's eyes. I walked over to calm her down thinking she was getting ready to have one of her tantrums, but she didn't. She was emotional, but calm. Vonna stood in front of her nervously not understanding Drekia's behavior. We all stood around looking confused; we had never seen this side of Drekia.

"Kids, will y'all please give me a few minutes with Mama?" Drekia said with her eyes set on Vonna. Aunt Dee's three kids left out the living room. Yella Boy and Zuri sat side by side on the couch confused as to what was going on. Aunt Dee and John, her husband, stood over by the fireplace. I stood beside Drekia waiting to hear what she had to say to Vonna.

"I don't remember getting attacked, but I remember every detail that led up to that moment. Me and Trina were hanging out on the corner down from her house. Maniac wanted me to ride with him. He said you wanted to fuck him, but he wanted to fuck me. I defended you and cussed him out, embarrassing him in front of his crew. He jumped out the car to whoop my ass, but me and Trina ran to her house. He tried to come in the house for me, but Trina's mama threatened to call the cops, so he left. Hours later I was worried that he might catch me walking home, so I called you to come get me. I told you what happened. Everyone knew how crazy Maniac was, even you. You told me you were at a bar and wasn't leaving. You said if he tries to whoop my ass to fuck him instead. I begged you to come get me, but you hung up on me," Drekia said with a trembling voice as tears rolled down her face.

"I was drunk," Vonna explained shamefully.

"You weren't drunk when you chose to walk away from me while I was in a coma. You left me there like I was nothing to you. All these years I thought you were working. Now, I know you were being a pathetic ass excuse for a parent. All the lies you told me about Drek not wanting me here anymore. That's the only reason I bought that house, thinking Drek was going to send me to a mental hospital. You made me pay you to stay there with me, had me thinking it was for the loss of income from your job. As my mother that birthed me, I will always have love for you. As a human being, I don't want or need you in my life," Drekia said wiping her tears away.

"You did this! I knew I shouldn't have left her in Switzerland with you!" Vonna screamed angrily at Aunt Dee. She charged toward Aunt Dee only to be put on her back by Aunt Dee's fist. I chuckled when I saw that her wig had fallen off her head.

"Dammmnnn!" Yella Boy barked jumping up off the sofa. John helped Vonna off the floor.

"Sister, I love you, but don't ever try me like that," Aunt Dee said staring at Vonna.

"Here you go, Aunt V," Yella Boy said trying to put Vonna's wig back on her head. I chuckled.

"Give me my shit," Vonna said snatching the wig from him.

"Don't be getting mad at me. You shouldn't be wearing that hot ass wig anyway. It's too damn hot for that. Be like Zuri, bald as hell," Yella Boy said to Vonna. Zuri rolled her eyes at him.

"I ain't lying. You is bald as fuck, but you pretty," he said to Zuri with a straight face, shrugging his shoulders.

"Boy, shut da fuck up. You always been slow as hell!" Vonna said furiously to Yella Boy. Drekia's tears weren't falling anymore. She giggled as Vonna tried to put on her wig. Vonna broke down and started crying, and Aunt Dee walked over to comfort her. I couldn't understand why Yella Boy was patting the top of Vonna's head. Zuri walked over and slapped his hand away.

"You can't comfort people like you do those damn dogs you breeding," Zuri told him. Me, Drekia and John laughed.

"I'm tired. I'm going to my old room to sleep," Drekia said smiling at me. She gave everyone a hug except Vonna. I didn't know if she would ever forgive Vonna, and I wasn't going to pressure her into forgiving her. Maybe that was something she could learn to do with counseling and therapy.

Aunt Dee and Vonna made up before Aunt Dee left. Yella Boy and Zuri said goodnight leaving me with Aunt Dee, Lil J and John. He had purchased Zelda's house and they would use it whenever they came to visit.

It had been a few hours since Zelda went upstairs, so while Aunt Dee was feeding Lil J, I went upstairs to check on her. When I walked in the bedroom, I broke out into a cold sweat. My heart felt like it was going to burst. Zelda had collapsed on the floor by the bed. I rushed to her to see that she was still conscious, but weak. She couldn't form a word to speak. I scooped her up in my arms and rushed downstairs.

"She collapsed," I said to Aunt Dee and John without stopping.

"Oh my God!" Aunt Dee screamed. I didn't have time for any questions. I broke every red light rushing to the hospital.

*****

I had called the ER to let them know I was on the way with a patient. When I arrived, they met me at the entrance with a gurney. I was so scared of losing her that I wouldn't let anyone touch her. I put her on the gurney and stayed with the gurney as they wheeled her inside the emergency entrance.

"Sir, we need to get some information on the patient," an elderly black woman said approaching me.

"Zelda Vandross. Look her up," I said not taking my eyes off Zelda.

"This is as far as you can go. The doctor will do everything he can for her," a short, white nurse said to me. That bitch must be out of her mind if she thought I wasn't going in the room with Zelda.

"You either move out my way or I put a bullet in your head," I warned her. She immediately moved out the way. I rushed to the room where they had taken Zelda. They were hooking her to machines and removing her blouse. I stood at the foot of the bed staring at her. The color had drained from her face and she could barely hold her eyes open.

"Dr. Bailon is on his way," the white nurse said walking in the room. She didn't come alone; she brought security with her. He was clearly younger than me and while he had height, he was paper thin. A strong gust of wind could knock him over.

"Man, you know you can't be in here. I just got this job. We both know you can whoop my ass, and I ain't 'bout to shoot you for wanting to be in here with yo wife. Let's help each other by walking out of here, so they can help her. Either we do it this way, or they gon' call the white police officers. We know how that will end," he said calmly.

I walked over and kissed Zelda on her forehead before walking out the room. After leaving the room, the security guard dapped me before going on about his business. I paced the floor impatiently waiting for someone to come tell me something. Dr. Bailon came walking down the hall while talking on his phone. I assumed the chart in his hand was Zelda's. He hadn't looked up to see me when he approached and bumped into me. I yoked him up by his neck leaving his feet dangling in the air.

"You better fix whatever da fuck is wrong with her. If you don't, I will kill everyone in yo family until it's your turn to die. Report this promise and your family will be dead by morning," I warned him with cold eyes. Fear oozed from his pores as I lowered him down to his feet.

"Save her life and I'm indebted to you for life," I promised.

"Yes sir, Mr. Jackson," he said hurrying away.

Next Day

Zelda

I woke up to the sounds of machines beeping. My body felt exhausted, but I didn't feel ill. I never realized how much all hospital rooms looked alike. I felt like I was in the same room as previously. Jedrek jumped up from the recliner when he saw my eyes opening. It felt like déjà vu. At least I didn't have the tube down my throat. I slowly sat up in the bed, and Jedrek held a cup of water for me to take a sip. The water was soothing to my dry throat.

"I guess I was more exhausted than I thought," I said smiling at him. His eyes looked sad, stressed and tired.

"How you feeling?" he asked brushing my wild hair from my face with his hand.

"I don't feel sick, just tired. Where's Lil J?" I asked.

"He's with Aunt Dee," he said.

"How long have I been here? Feels like I've been sleep for days."

"Only a day. Dr. Bailon ran some test. Once everything is negative, he said you can go home," Jedrek said.

I looked at the blood pressure monitor and started to worry because my blood pressure and heart rate were low. They weren't as low as they were before, but they weren't where they needed to be. Jedrek saw the concern in my eyes.

"He's thinking you need stronger meds for your heart muscles," he said trying to comfort me. That sounded like a logical explanation, so I breathed a sigh of relief. Once he prescribed me stronger meds, I could get out of there, or so I thought.

"In the meantime, I'll fill you in on what happened after you went upstairs," he said pulling a chair beside my bed and taking a seat. I was in shock at Drekia's revelation. Drekia loved Vonna, so I knew it hurt to face the reality of who her mother was. I laughed when he told me about Yella Boy's antics.

"I want another baby when Lil J turns one," I said smiling at him. He laughed. I loved these moments when he was completely happy.

"You just wanna fuck all the time," he said.

"Yea that too, but while I was asleep, I had a dream. We had four kids. They were all a year apart, two boys and three girls," I said.

"That's five," he said.

"We gon' adopt one," I told him smiling.

"What about expanding your law firm?"

"I'm going into family law," I informed him. I had been thinking about it ever since he asked me to help him with Drekia. I never considered how important family legal matters were. Things could get messy without the proper legal procedures and documents.

Dr. Bailon walked into the room interrupting our conversation. He looked nervous and scared.

"Chill out, doc. She still breathing," Jedrek said. He gave Jedrek a smile and a nod of the head. This was the reason I didn't want him knowing about the surgery before I had it. It was obvious he threatened Dr. Bailon. Dr. Bailon's dark skin complexion looked pale.

"What's the diagnosis?" I asked. He glanced at Jedrek like a little boy scared to speak.

"Don't worry about him. He's going to be on his best behavior." I rolled my eyes at Jedrek.

"Go head," Jedrek said to him.

Dr. Bailon cleared his throat. "The damage to your arteries weakened your heart muscles tremendously; more than we thought. We repaired the damage to the arteries, but they aren't strong enough. It's causing your muscles to weaken."

"I have to have another surgery?" I asked exhaustedly. The look he gave me scared me. I knew it was more than just another surgery to repair damage to my arteries.

"Mr. Jackson, I'm sorry it has come to this," he said looking at Jedrek instead of me.

"Fuck him! This is my life! What do we have to do to fix this?" I screamed at him. He jumped when Jedrek stood up and walked over to him.

"What we gotta do?" Jedrek asked calmly. He looked over Jedrek's shoulders at me.

"Ms. Vandross, we have to put you on the list for an organ donor. Your heart is weakening. Medications can only strengthen it for a while," he said regretfully.

Jedrek immediately looked back at me. His eyes were filled with so much fear and sadness. Tears instantly filled my eyes. My life was just beginning; I wasted so many years of life fighting to never give my heart and soul to a man. Now, I couldn't imagine my life without the love and joy I felt with him and Lil J. Waiting for a heart donor could take forever, and by the look in Dr. Bailon's eyes, I didn't have a lifetime to wait. I closed my eyes and said a quick prayer.

"How long do I have?" I asked.

"I'm going to make finding a donor my priority."

"That's not what she asked you," Jedrek said calmly but firmly.

"With the medication I'm prescribing, there's not an amount of time I can give you, but your heart muscles will continue to weaken. It is your right to seek a second opinion," he explained. Dr. Bailon was too scared for his life to come to us without medical facts about my health. I was going to take his advice, but I knew in my heart I'd be given the same diagnosis.

We live to die. Every life has a time limit. No one knew when it was their turn to leave this earth, but I had the advantage because I could prepare for my last days. I was going to stay optimistic about getting a heart transplant, but I was going to live my every day like it was my last day to enjoy loving my family and friends.

"When can I go home?" I asked. Jedrek and Dr. Bailon looked at me like I was crazy.

"Ain't no going home until we get you a heart," Jedrek said staring at me.

"Mr. Jackson, I understand your concern, but she doesn't have to stay confined to the hospital. I just recommend taking her meds and continuing a healthy, stress free, happy life until we find Ms. Vandross a heart," Dr. Bailon stated.

"Then I recommend you go find one," Jedrek demanded to Dr. Bailon. His demand sounded more like a threat than a suggestion.

"A nurse will bring your prescriptions. After that, you are free to go home. I will call you in a couple of days for a follow up appointment. In the meantime, I will work relentlessly until we have you a heart," he assured me. I forced a smile and nodded my head.

"I will stop by your office before I leave," Jedrek told him before Dr. Bailon left the room.

"Jedrek, please stop threatening him. That's not going to solve anything," I said firmly. He sat back down in the chair and dropped his head. He felt useless and defeated, because he couldn't protect or fix this for me.

"Jedrek, look at me," I said softly. He slowly lifted his head. It broke my heart to see him this way.

"All I need from you is love," I told him.

Two Weeks Later

Crue

"Look at you looking all classy and chic," Zelda said when she opened the door. I was totally shocked when I saw her. She looked completely healthy, and her face was glowing with radiant, smooth chocolate beauty. She didn't look like a woman that needed a new heart. When she called me a couple of days ago, I was completely crushed. Nothing could take away the pain I felt for causing her illness.

"You sure it's okay with Drek?" I asked. She didn't ask that I come over, she demanded it. I wanted to see her, Lil J and Drekia, but I knew how much Drek hated me.

"Girl get in here," she said, gently grabbing my hand. She wrapped her arms around me and held me. Her hug wasn't just a greeting. It was a warm, loving and forgiving hug. I clung to her, squeezing her tight and asking for forgiveness without speaking a word.

"Where's Quay?" she asked after breaking our embrace.

"She had to work. She told me to tell you she'll come by soon," I told her.

"Come on, so you can see your little cousin," she said pulling me farther into the house and down the hall. When we walked in the den, I froze. I didn't know Drek would be here. He was sitting in a big recliner, playing with Lil J. Zelda squeezed my hand assuring me it was okay for me to be here.

"Go, hold him," she said smiling at me. I slowly walked over and stood in front of Drek. He never looked up at me while I made silly faces and sounds at Lil J. Lil J cooed and laughed as I played with him. He was the perfect baby in my eyes.

"Can I hold him?" I asked Jedrek nervously. He glanced at me before holding Lil J up for me to hold. I wrapped my arms around his soft, chubby body giving a gentle snug. I sat down on the sofa and enjoyed playing with my little cousin. He was the sweetest baby.

"Can I get some love too," Drekia said walking into the den. I jumped up excitedly and passed Lil J to Zelda. Me and Drekia screamed with excitement as we hugged. Drekia looked the same, but something about her had changed. She held herself with confidence, assurance and style. Jedrek whispered in Zelda's ear before kissing her on the forehead and took Lil J from her arms. He walked over to Drekia.

"Slow yo ass down in that car. I heard how you be driving fast as hell," he said sternly. She giggled and waved him off. He gave me a head nod and left the den.

We all started talking about life. Zelda and Drekia's positivity about their struggles made my worries feel silly. The only problem I had was getting my life together and feeling something for my best friend's boyfriend. Those were things I could control. Vanity came over and joined our ladies' day, and we sat and talked for hours. I wished Quay had been there to listen to some of the jewels all the women gave me.

*****

I forgot expensive wine hit different. I had only drunk half a glass and it had me tipsy. Vanity dropped me off at the hotel on her way home, because they didn't want me to take the chance of driving myself. When I walked into my hotel room, Chike was relaxed on my bed.

"How did you get in here?" I asked angrily snatching my notepad from his hand. I had been writing down the goals I wanted to achieve. That was my personal business, and he had no right to read it.

"I told you to answer your damn phone when I call you," he said sitting up on the side of the bed.

"I've been busy," I lied. I had intentionally ignored all his calls. It wasn't that I wanted to, but I was trying to fight temptation. Quay told me about how close they were getting; she believed he was finally falling for her.

"I see," he said glancing at my notepad. He grabbed me by the waist and pulled me down on the bed. I wrestled to get up, but he pinned me down by rolling on top of me.

"Man chill out. I ain't trying to make you do anything you don't wanna do," he said staring into my eyes. I stopped fighting. He sat up, resting his back against the headboard.

"It's against the law to break into peoples' rooms," I said rolling my eyes at him. He chuckled and took my notepad that was now lying beside me.

"What's up with this?" he asked. I didn't know why I felt embarrassed about him seeing the things I wanted to accomplish.

"You can't read?" I asked rolling my eyes at him.

He laughed which was rare. When I first met him, Chike hardly talked and never smiled. It was still rare to see him smile, but now he talked quite a bit when he was around me. He patted the space beside him on the bed.

"Sit right here," he said. I reluctantly slid beside him with my back against the headboard.

"Get married to a rich man, have a family and travel the world," he said reading a few things from my list.

"Yea, what's wrong with those?" I asked. He shrugged his shoulders.

"Nothing, I'm pretty sure that's what every woman wants. What is Cruella gonna do to make these things happen?" he asked. I didn't have an answer for that.

"In order to achieve goals, you have to have a plan. To plan, you gotta study and research," he said.

"So, I should be researching how to find a rich man?" I asked laughing.

"Nah, you should be learning yourself. Correcting things within yourself in order to grow to achieve your goals. Admitting your flaws is the beginning of becoming a better you," he told me.

"And who told you this, Dr. Phil?" I asked jokingly.

He laughed. "Life. I was a rebellious teenager. I gave Ma hell until I realized I had to make changes in myself or shit was gon' stay the same."

"So, my list should start with things I want to change about myself to achieve my goals?" I asked. He nodded his head.

I turn to the notepad and stared at the blank page. "Can I ask you something?"

"Yea," Chike answered.

"What's something you would change about me?" I asked shyly.

"That shouldn't matter. I ain't rich," he said smiling at me. I laughed and nudged him.

"I'm serious."

His gazed at me with a straight face. "When I first met you, I would say everything. After getting to know you, the only thing I would change about you is the hold you have on me."

My mouth slowly opened releasing a deep breath. We sat there a few seconds staring at each other. He leaned over and stroked his wet tongue across my bottom lip. The thud between my thighs pounded harder than my heartbeat. Our mouths locked together for a heated, passionate kiss. I broke it before it went any further.

"What are we doing, Chike? You telling me to write down my faults. Well, this is one of them. How can I be a better person while fucking my best friend's boyfriend?"

"I'm not her boyfriend. Quay knows that. She's living with Ma until she gets her own place. I ain't trying to pressure you into doing anything, but you know this feeling just ain't gon' go away," he said.

"She didn't tell me that she was living with your ma," I said surprised by his revelation.

"I felt like her living with me was giving her the wrong impression. Plus, I have Special at my house right now," he said.

"What about Special?" I asked.

"She trying to kick that shit. Rehab ain't the place for her, and she can't go back to her parents' house," he explained.

"Do you still love Special? Does she still love you?" I asked. I didn't want to continue this with him knowing they still loved each other.

"Nah, I got love for her as the mother of my child. Only thing she loves right now is her next hit. She's been sober for a couple of weeks, but that shit is hard for her. The withdrawals ain't no joke," he told me.

"I know. My daddy has been a crackhead for as long as I can remember. He tried kicking it a few times but was never able to do it. They need twenty-four-hour supervision this early into withdrawal. Who's with her now?" I asked.

"Ma and Krysta. I thought spending a little time with Krysta would keep her motivated to stay clean."

I smiled. "That was smart and nice. If you ever need someone to sit with her, I will. I hate what that shit does to people. I can tell she was once a beautiful girl."

"You'd do that?" he asked shockingly.

"Yea, why not?" I asked shrugging my shoulders.

"You ain't scared she gon' be getting this dick that have you trembling like you having a seizure," he said grabbing his crotch.

I laughed while getting off the bed. "Boy, please. That dick ain't even all that."

"Swear it ain't?" he asked getting off the bed. He started walking to my side of the bed, but I ran toward the bathroom. His strong arms lifted me off the floor before I could escape, and he threw me on the bed.

"Tell me how good I give it to you," he said tickling me with no mercy. I pleaded for him to stop as I laughed until I had to confess.

"Okay okay! I lied; it's the best I ever had," I said honestly. He finally had mercy on me and stood straight up. My eyes zoomed in on the big bulge in his jeans.

"You want some right now?" I bit my bottom lip and nodded my head, wanting him in the worse way.

"I need to shower. I'm sweaty," I said sitting up on the bed. We sat by Drek's pool and sipped wine. Even though fall weather was coming in, it was still hot.

"I like you sweaty," he said smiling at me. I laughed and pushed him out the way.

I went inside the bathroom and removed my clothes. The water from the shower steamed up the windows when I got the right temperature. Chike pushed the shower curtain back revealing his dark chocolate, rippled abs and rock-hard dick. He licked his lips before stepping in behind me. He took my soapy sponge from me and bathed every inch of my body. Wetness flowed from my core as his hands massaged my body. He dropped the sponge and massaged my breasts while his tongue lick, sucked and bit my neck and shoulders.

"Aaaaahhh," I whimpered softly, resting my back against his chest. I spread my legs begging him to fill my insides. When I reached behind me for his treasure, he turned my body, so I was facing the opposite end of the shower. I placed the palms of my hand against the shower wall when he pressed my lower back to bend me over. Palming and spreading my ass cheeks, he placed his rod at my entrance.

"*Oomph!*" He grunted loudly sliding inside my wetness. My slippery walls opened and welcomed him inside. Slow, deep strokes sent chills of sensation through my body. His hand slid between my pussy lips, massaging my clit. My hips synchronized with the twirling of his fingers. Digging his shaft deeper inside me, his girth sex grew, filling my tunnel until I cried out in ecstasy. My soft moans turn to screams of pleasure.

"Ooooohhh Chiikkke!" I cried out as he drilled his dick against my g-spot. He dug his fingers in my ass cheeks spreading them apart. I let go of the wall, spread my feet farther apart, and grabbed my ankles.

"Fuuuuccckkk!" Chike barked as he glided deeper inside. I clamped my walls around his shaft, wanting to feel everything he was giving me. His head was pressing merciless against my spot.

"Come for me," he moaned feeling my orgasm building. He didn't change his stroke. It stayed steady and addictive. His finger on my clit, pulsating dick in my pussy and thumb in my ass had my juices seeping down my inner thighs. His pelvis slapped against my wet ass until neither of us could hold back.

"Ooooohhh! Shiiiittt! I'm commminnnggg!" I screamed as saliva spilled from my mouth. My body trembled uncontrollably as waves of blissful pleasure flowed through me.

"Aaaarrrrggghhhh!" Chike roared coming with me.

We literally fucked each other to sleep.

*****

The next morning, I could barely climb out the bed. The soreness between my thighs caused me to walk slow and awkward to the bathroom. I thought Chike had left, but he was taking a piss when I opened the bathroom door.

"Hi," I said smiling at him nervously.

"You good?" he asked.

"Yea, I'm going to talk to Quay. Regardless of what happens between me and you, she's gotta accept what isn't happening between you and her," I said leaning against the bathroom door entrance. I smiled at him when I saw his dick getting hard.

"Calm that down. I can barely walk," I said smiling. He laughed when he realized he was getting hard. I went to answer my phone when it rang.

"Is my got damn son with you?" Shyma screamed through the phone when I answered. I immediately gave Chike the phone. He put her on speaker knowing she was pissed.

"My bad, Ma. I got caught up; I'm on the way."

"Boy, if you don't get yo ass here. I missed a good dicking down last night fooling with you. I had to pop Special's ass in the mouth to get her to calm down. Brang yo ass home. Got damn girl must got silver and gold between her legs that you can't find yo way home," she rambled angrily before ending the call. Me and Chike covered our mouths to keep from laughing out loud.

"She really hates me now," I said. She called my phone again and told Chike to put her on speaker.

"And if you hurt my son, I'm gon' fuck you up," she said ending the call again. We burst out laughing. I hated to see him go, but I knew he had things to handle. I was late for my housekeeping duties anyway.

Three Days Later

Quay

Everything irritated my soul. I hated staying here with Shyma, because she was bossy and rude. All she wanted to do was give me orders like she was my mother. Even the sounds of Chike's whining daughter, Krysta, irritated me. She was a spoiled child that thought everyone was supposed to kiss her ass. If she was my child, I would spoil her rotten, but she's not my child to spoil. If they allowed me, I would discipline her, so she wouldn't cry so much.

They weren't the reason for my mood. Crue was the blame for that. I watched Chike go inside the hotel where she was staying the other night. I called his phone the entire night only to be sent to voicemail. I sat outside the hotel and watched him walk out the next morning. Crue was fucking the man I wanted, and she didn't deserve him. I was the good girl with a good head on her shoulders. I knew what I wanted out of life; I was wifey material. Crue only wanted money, and her way of getting money was to use men. I hadn't seen Chike since I moved out. Today was my day off, so I was going to surprise him. I had made some homemade brownies for Special to take over to his house. I didn't like her, but I had to pretend to be supportive if I wanted Chike.

"What are you doing?" I shouted angrily at Krysta. She was sitting at the kitchen table digging in my pan of brownies. She jumped nearly falling out the chair. I had left them out to cool before cutting them. Now, they are ruined. I walked over and grabbed her by the arm. She immediately started whining.

"You got about a half a breath to get your hands off my grandchild, before I take that same breath from you," Shyma said walking into the kitchen. Her mean eyes turned deadly. My hands immediately released Krysta's arm.

"Go play in the backyard," Shyma said to Krysta never taking her eyes off me.

"I sorry, Gana. I thought they was mine," she said looking up at Shyma.

Shyma kneeled to Krysta's eye level. "Never touch things without asking. We've had this discussion. We will bake some brownies later for you. Now, apologize to Ms. Quaysha for eating her brownies."

Krysta turned to face me. "I'm sorry, Ms. Quaysha. I will share mine with you."

I forced a smile before Krysta ran out the kitchen. Shyma stepped in my space. Her skin was blemish free and beautiful. She reminded me of a young Naomi Campbell, but the hood version.

"I'm sorry. I've been under a lot of stress. I didn't mean to lose my temper with her," I said remorsefully.

"A child always needs discipline. One thing I learned is to never discipline a child with the stress of life on your shoulders. Never put your hands on a child until you have your emotions under control. I agreed to let you stay in my home for my son, but that agreement is off. You gotta go. I don't mean in a few days, couple of weeks, or months. Your time is up. I wish the best for you, but it's time to go."

She didn't give me a chance to respond. I stood in the middle of the kitchen wondering how I was going to fix this. Chike would never forgive me for putting my hands on his child without his permission. It was his and Crue's fault I was in this state of mind. They were to blame for me losing my temper with Krysta. I packed my things and checked into a hotel close to my job. I couldn't go to Chike's house now, so I decided to visit Crue. I wanted her to feel the guilt of what she was doing to me.

*****

"You like this bag?" Crue asked holding up a cute Hermes bag.

"Yea, but I can't afford that. I need to find a cheap apartment. I don't think you can either unless you still finessing men," I said. I was hoping she would tell me she was still up to her old tricks, so I could tell Chike.

"Nope, I'm being a good girl. I'm just window shopping. I haven't bought anything expensive in a long time. Trying to be smart with my pennies," she said.

"Me too," I said as we walked out the store. We made small talk as we made our way to the food court. We sat at a table with our bourbon chicken and fried rice that we ordered from Mandarin Express.

"You look like you've got a lot on your mind. Everything okay?" Crue asked worriedly. It was my time to perform. I mustered up a few tears to fill my eyes.

"I think Chike is getting back with Special. He moved me out to move her in. He says he's helping her get off drugs, but I know they're messing around. He was supposed to pick me up from work the other night, but he never showed up. I've been so upset that I took my frustration out on Krysta. I yelled at her and grabbed her arm. Shyma got so upset and threw me out. Now, I know I'll never stand a chance with Chike. I just want a chance to prove I can love him like no one else can. I can't have that chance because he's sneaking around with Special or someone else."

Crue dropped her head. I knew the shame and guilt was eating her up the way I wanted it to. If she was a loyal friend, this would make her stay away from him.

"I'm sorry, Quay, but as your best friend, I have to be honest with you. It doesn't matter if it's someone else or not; Chike isn't into you that way. He never has been. I knew it, but I was hoping things could change; they haven't. Even if he was, putting your hands on Krysta ruined any chance you might've had with him. It's time to let it go and move on," she said with pathetic ass eyes. I was beyond heated with her. She was supposed to encourage me and give me advice on how to get him to fall in love with me.

"How do you know? You've never been in love or had a man who loved you. You've only fucked men for money. That ain't love. That's what almost ended Zelda's life and mine. I should've never listened to you about trying to be hard with Chike. You probably wanted him for yourself since Quan was fucking you for pennies."

I didn't mean to go overboard, but it was too late to take the words back. Crue's eyes turned from shame to rage. My words cut her deep, as they should.

"I know you're hurt and angry about my words, so I'm gon' let that slide, Quay. You have every right to be angry, but not about my words or jeopardizing your life," she said.

My eyes widened. "You were the one that convinced me to go with you to rob Khalil. If I hadn't, I wouldn't have been kidnapped and raped."

"Yes, I did convince you, but not force you. I told you I would understand if you didn't want to do it. You agreed to come with me on your own free will," she told me. She was right. I was so desperate to get away from our hometown I went along with her.

"What do I have the right to be angry about if not that?" I asked frustrated with this conversation.

She dropped her head again. I sat back in my seat and waited for her response. When she finally looked up, her eyes were full of tears.

"I didn't want it to happen. I tried to fight it, but I couldn't. We've been best friends for so long. I don't want this to tear us apart, but I don't know if we can get past what I did," she said as her fake tears started to fall.

"I forgave you for the Khalil mess. I shouldn't blame you because I made the choice to come with you," I said.

She shook her head. "It's not about Khalil. It's about Chike."

She admitted to my face what I already knew. I never wanted to hear Crue admit to fucking Chike. She was supposed to sympathize with what I was going through and leave him alone for good this time. The ache in my heart was telling me to leap across the table and walk the dog on her, instead I broke out into a controllable cry. Everyone sitting around was staring at us. Crue pleaded and begged me to forgive her and to stop crying. I didn't stop until I heard her say our friendship meant more than anything to her.

"Thank you for choosing our friendship over Chike. I forgive you," I said wiping my tears away.

"Quaysha, I love you, but I'm not choosing one over the other. I have no right, but I'm asking you to understand. I know I can't have your blessing," she said.

I lost it. I reached across the table and slapped the spit out of Crue's mouth. She jumped up and punched me in the jaw. Crue and I were fighters, so we didn't believe in pulling hair. We tied up throwing fists at each other, knocking over tables and chairs. I could taste the blood in my mouth from my busted lip. We didn't stop until security pulled us apart and we were thrown out of the mall. Crue left me there since I rode with her. I called an Uber to take me to my hotel room. I didn't know how, but I was going to pay her back for what she did.

Jedrek

"No! I do not want a heart that way!" Zelda screamed at me. She overheard me talking with Echon earlier about finding a heart for her on the black market.

"Why da fuck not? The person that it belongs to don't need it anymore. It's just got damn sitting there," I asked her angrily.

"That person was murdered so someone could get their organs. We don't know the pain that family suffered from losing their loved one. I don't want to walk around with someone's heart that I know nothing about," she said.

"She's right, Jedrek. Who knows what kind of person that heart belonged to? They could've been a serial killer or something," Drekia said walking into the kitchen.

I left the kitchen, not wanting to admit they were right. I just wanted to save her life. She was acting as if she didn't have a care in the world while her heart was weakening every day. You wouldn't know that by looking at her, because she looked as if she could live forever. Her weight was back up and she was making my dick hard every time I looked at her. Dr. Bailon said we could have a normal sex life, but I didn't want to stress her heart. He didn't know how I fucked Zelda. If he did, he probably would advise us not to have sex.

I went to work out to relieve stress and to clear my mind. After I was done, I relaxed in the Jacuzzi. Before long Zelda walked outside wearing a two piece that stressed my dick.

"Before you ask about the baby, Drekia is feeding him and putting him to sleep," she said getting in the Jacuzzi and straddling my lap.

"You dying and all you can think about is fucking me," I said. She started winding her hips causing her pussy to rub against my dick.

"If I have to leave this world, I want all the dick I can get from you," she said smiling at me. Her nonchalant demeanor about her life enraged me. I stood up causing her to fall into the Jacuzzi. I yanked her up by her arm when she went under water. She pushed me hard in the chest, making me almost fall. I caught my balance and sat back down.

"That wasn't funny," she said angrily brushing her drenched hair from her face.

I chuckled. "I ain't mean to do that shit."

"You don't find me attractive anymore, because I'm sick?" she asked sadly.

"Zelda, your heart is weak. I ain't trying to take chances and make it worse."

Instead of replying to my comment, she left me in the Jacuzzi in deep thought. I remembered Dr. Bailon saying she needed to stay stress free. When I walked into the bedroom, Zelda was stretched across the bed, naked, massaging *my* pussy with a vibrator.

"Get that bullshit away from my pussy," I barked snatching it from her hand. She gasped for her breath, frightened by my outburst.

"Doc said stress free. I'm fucking stressed. If you won't help me relieve it, that thing will," she said reaching for it. I pulled my hand away throwing the vibrator across the room.

"Lay down," I demanded. She smiled and stretch out like an eagle soaring.

Her fingers slid between her wet pussy lips as she watched me take off my swim trunks. I kneeled and pulled her ass to the edge of the bed. Her juicy pussy made my mouth water. I kept telling myself to be gentle with her, to not overwork her heart muscles. My fingers spread her fat pussy lips exposing her soaked center. She whimpered softly when my tongue lapped up her juices. I tongue kissed her pussy slow and gentle while her hips twirled and bucked, spreading her juicy over my face.

"I want more, give me all of it, Jedrek," she begged.

She wrapped her legs around my neck and grabbed the back of my head. My face was buried between her lips. Her hips gyrated, making my tongue taste every inch of her sweet pussy. I sucked on her swollen clit, making her scream out my name. My dick was throbbing from the taste of her and the sound of her cries for more of my tongue. I slipped my tongue inside her dripping, wet tunnel, tongue fucking her pussy. My hands grabbed her soft ass cheeks lifting them off the bed. Her wetness had seeped into the sheets. My tongue licked and slurped from her pussy to her ass until her legs tightened around my neck. Wrapping my arms around her thighs, I pulled them from around my neck. I flipped over sitting on the floor with my head leaning on the bed. Zelda's pussy was still in my face, but she was positioned on all fours.

"Feed me," I growled like a caveman slapping her ass cheeks. I wanted her to baptize me with her sweet fluids. She saturated my face the way I loved as she rode my face. The more she moaned and cried, the harder my dick got. I could feel myself getting ready to come with her.

"Fuck, this pussy juicy," I groaned as her fluids spilled down the sides of my mouth. Slurping wets sounds rang in my ear until her body quivered.

"I'm coooommminnnngggg! Shhhhiiiittt! Fuuuucccckkk!" I had to turn my head to the side to keep from drowning in her orgasm. Her juices splattered on my face like a busted pipe. She whimpered and moaned riding out the blissful wave as she fell over on the bed onto her back. I quickly stood up praying she was okay. I looked down at her as she lay on the bed twitching with her eyes rolled back in her head.

"Fuck! I knew we shouldn't have done this shit!" I barked. She looked like she was having a seizure. I was caught off guard by her soft moans. She started massaging her breast with one hand as the other slipped between her thighs.

"Please fuck me," she pleaded with low eyes.

When my brick hard dick jumped, I looked down at it. My cum was on my thigh from coming while eating her out. I flipped her over and positioned her on all fours. I got on the bed on my knees. She looked back at me biting her bottom lip and twirling her ass. She was purposefully fucking with me to make me give it to her the hard way. This was where I controlled her, but she was in control. Zelda laid her breasts on the bed making the perfect arch in her back, the way I taught her. A low growl slipped from me as I leaned over and grabbed a handful of her hair.

"GGGGGRRRRRR!" I growled ramming my dick inside her tight, wet tunnel. She cried out in ecstasy and pain as her walls grabbed hold of my shaft. When she tried running from my dick inside her, I pulled her up by her hair pressing her back against my chest.

"I'm gon' make you regret begging for this," I whispered in her ear.

I pushed her head back down in the bed and planted the soles of my feet into the bed. My body was in a sitting rammed position with my dick buried deep inside her. Sloppy, gushy, wet sounds echoed through the room as I hammered in and out of her. When she came, her creaminess coated my dick. I flipped her over and pushed her legs up to her head, burying myself back inside her. She wasn't pleading for mercy. Zelda was begging me for more. The way she was taking my dick was driving me insane. I glanced down to see her cream covering the base of my dick. Her nails were digging and clawing into my skin as I pounded inside heaven. Our bodies were covered in sweat, but I couldn't stop until I gave her everything she wanted. She was coming back to back. I came once inside of her, and my dick was still aching for more. She was mumbling as I continued to beat my dick inside her tunnel.

"I don't wanna die," she moaned softly. I stopped and stared down at her. "I love you so much," she said with tears streaming down the sides of her face. Cold chills traveled through my sweaty body. She was all I needed in this world. I let her legs go and rested my body on top of hers, staring down at her.

"Love ain't a strong enough word for how you make me feel. You won't die. We got a lifetime together," I assured her.

"Not if you keep fucking me like that," she said smiling at me. I laughed.

"You asked for it."

She laughed. I made love to her until we came together. The rest of our night was spent planning our future and discussing the places we wanted to visit alone and with our kids. Before I let her die, I would give her my heart.

Three Weeks Later

Chike

Crue sat across from me smiling like a shy schoolgirl. She had been sad and depressed, since her fight with Quay. Most of her time was spent working or with Zelda and Drekia. It was like she had been avoiding me. I didn't want to put pressure on her, but a nigga hadn't seen her in two weeks. The last time I saw her, she asked me to stay away for a while, and I honored her request. I couldn't say I wasn't happy when she called me a couple of days ago. I had been working the streets, hustling my side businesses and helping Special. She had come a long way in five weeks, but she still had a long rode for her.

"Why you acting shy and shit?" I asked her. She shrugged her shoulders.

"I've never been on this kind of date," she said shamefully.

"What kind of date you mean?"

"I mean I've had men take me out to eat and things like that. The difference with this date is I'm not trying to get in your pockets. I've never been on a date with a guy I actually liked," she said smiling.

"What about your ex-boyfriend?"

She rolled her eyes. "Where I'm from niggas don't take females on dates. They take you to Netflix and chill. Next thing you know you the main bitch."

I laughed. "I know you been feeling down, so I wanted to make this night different."

"Different?"

"You lost your best friend because of fucking with me. I just wanna show you it wasn't just about fucking you. I can't replace her, but I would like to see where this can go," I told her.

A big smile spread across her face. "Who are you?"

"I mean at first it was a sexual attraction. We were wrong as hell for letting temptation get us to this point, but it's more than that now," I told her.

"No, I don't mean that. I just never thought you were this kind of guy. You were so disrespectful and quiet. I'm just surprised to see this side of you," she said smiling.

"Ma preached to me about respecting women for as long as I can remember. She also told me to guard my heart, because it's some trifling women that don't deserve respect from a man. I've never been scared to let a female know I'm feeling her," I told her.

"So, you feeling me?" she asked flirting with me.

"Nah, yo pussy just good," I said smiling. She laughed and threw her napkin at me.

"How many girls have you taken on dates?"

"A few," I answered honestly. I had dated a few girls since Special, but nothing serious.

"How did you know I love this restaurant?" she asked looking around at the ambience.

"Special told me," I confessed. Crue had come over a couple of times and sat with Special when Ma wasn't available. Crue shared a lot with her about dealing with her dad being on drugs. She was the one that suggested I take Crue on a date. Special knew of my involvement with Crue and liked the friendship Crue had with Krysta.

"She's really trying to stay clean. I told her we can go shopping next weekend. She's gaining weight and needs some clothes," she said. I nodded my head. She sat quietly playing over her food.

"Has she called you?" she asked looking up at me. Her eyes were full of sadness. I knew she was missing her best friend.

"Nah, maybe she went back home," I replied.

"No, she hates that place. She wouldn't go back there. I know we can't be friends again, but I want to know she's okay. We came here for a better life together. Now, look at us," she said full of sorrow. "I can't do this, Chike. No matter how right this feels. This is wrong on so many levels. Please just take me back to my room," she said standing up.

I threw a few bills on the table to cover our tab and chased behind her as she rushed out the restaurant. We stood in front of the building until the valet brought my car. The ride back to her hotel room was quiet. When I pulled in front of the hotel, she sat in the car quietly. I wasn't going to force myself in her life. I could tell how hard this was for her and I didn't want to make it harder.

"You are a nice guy that deserves someone who has their shit together. My life is a mess and probably always will be. Karma is a bitch, and I have to pay for all the wrongs I've done. You don't need my energy around you or your beautiful daughter. I have to make amends for my poor choices. I can't call them mistakes, because I knew what I was doing. I can honestly say you've been the best thing that happened to me since I've been here. Thanks for being a friend to me."

She unbuckled her seatbelt and kissed me softly on the lips. Before she could pull away, I sucked her tongue into my mouth with a wet, sloppy kiss. I didn't want to let her go, but I knew this was something she needed to do for herself. She finally pulled away, resting her forehead against mine.

"This ain't over," I whispered against her lips. I watched her until she entered the hotel lobby.

*****

"Hi," Quay said opening her room door. I regretted calling her the moment the door opened, and she was wearing a sexy lingerie. Something told me coming here was only going to make matters worse between her and Crue.

"What up?" I walked into the room. No point in turning away now. Maybe I could talk some sense into her. I walked over and sat on the sofa.

"Go put on some clothes, Quay. That ain't why I'm here," I said. I couldn't deny how sexy she was looking. Her long legs stood tall with a small gap between her thighs; her breasts were pushed together making them appear bigger than they were.

"Why are you here?" she asked disappointed.

"I came to apologize. I ended things between us in a fucked-up way. I've always been straight up with you. When you caught feelings, I should've ending things. I apologize for that. I was wrong."

"It's not your fault. Crue has always been that way. Anytime she meets a man with money she tries to fuck him. I never thought she would do me like that though. I was so hurt. I didn't mean to fight her, but I was so angry. I can forgive you for sleeping with her. Let's just start over," she said trying to straddle my lap.

I grabbed her around the waist and sat her back down on the sofa. "That apology wasn't about Crue. But I apologize for the way I handled things with Crue. I'm the blame for it happening as much as her. She's fucked up behind this and worried about you. You can forgive and still wanna fuck with me but close your best friend out of your life? I'm going to be honest with you. I'm sorry for the way things went down with Crue, but not that it happened. She's the one that's sorry it happened."

She jumped up and tried to slap me, but I caught her wrist. She jerked away from me and walked over to the door. "Get out! She gon' do you like she does every other nigga."

I stood up and walked out the room. I turned to face her and apologize again, but she spoke first.

"By the way, Quan's dick was better than yours anyway," she said slamming the door in my face. She shocked me with that bit of information. As I walked to the elevator, I couldn't help but laugh at her confession.

A Month Later

Zelda

Jedrek drove quietly while holding my hand tightly. Neither of us knew what to say to the other. The sun was shining bright on this beautiful fall day, but there was a dark cloud looming over my head. My heart was weakening, and I didn't have a donor. If I had to leave this earth, I wanted my time here to be filled with love and happiness. I never confided in him about my body feeling tired over the past week. The month before that had been incredible.

I hated that I had wasted so many years of my life chasing my goals instead of my happiness. Work wasn't an option for me right now, so I recommended most of my clients to my colleagues. Things could happen in your life to make you realize what was truly important.

"I don't want anyone to know about this," I said glancing at him.

He didn't look at me, but I saw his jawline twitch. Before my doctor's appointment, we argued about seeking a heart on the black market. I was still strongly against it.

He released my hand and tightened his hand around the steering wheel.

Still not a word from him, until we pulled into the driveway of our home. He finally looked at me with his eyes full of sorrow.

"Why you wanna die?"

"I don't want to die, Jedrek. But if God puts it in the universe, I'm willing to accept it," I explained to him.

"Fuck God! I've killed many, but here I am healthy. What kind of God would let something like this happen to a person like you?" he said angrily.

"I don't know, but I believe whatever happens has a purpose. Somethings we can't control," I said. A loud roar of thunder vibrated the car as rain started to pour down, but the sun was still shining bright.

He chuckled. "I remember the first time I saw you at my restaurant. I knew yo sassy ass was gon' be trouble for me."

I laughed. "I wanted to hate you so bad, but you controlled my body, mind and heart."

"I knew I had to for you to be mine. You wasn't falling for no weak nigga. I tried to break you, so I wouldn't love you. But you were adamant about not being a doormat for me to walk over. The one thing I didn't expect was you controlling my heart," he confessed.

"You were such an asshole," I said smiling.

He placed the palm of his hand on the side of my face. "I ain't giving up. You gave me a happiness I never wanted."

I kissed the palm of his hand as he wiped the tear that slid down my cheek. Suddenly, the rain stopped, and a beautiful rainbow was over the house. Jedrek gave me that look that sent chills through me.

"You need to eat something," he said smiling at me.

"Let me find out you really are a werewolf," I said smiling back at me. He laughed remembering her reaction to meeting Clyde.

We never made it inside of the house. I straddled his lap and rode him until we exploded. It was never just sex with Jedrek. The colors from the rainbow exploded like fireworks inside my head. I was still straddling his lap when Drekia tapped on the foggy window. Jedrek lowered the window enough to see her eyes.

"Y'all just nasty," she said turning her nose up at us. We laughed.

"What up?" Jedrek asked.

"I got tired of sitting in the house waiting for the diagnosis. How did it go?" Drekia asked looking at me with concern.

"Everything is good. My heart is getting stronger," I lied. I didn't want to feel anyone's pity. This was the time for me to enjoy life to the fullest, not to be treated like a fragile piece of art. Drekia jumped with joy.

"Let's celebrate!" she shouted.

"Can we get decent and get out the car?" Jedrek asked. She waved him off and walked back into the house. He gave me a soft kiss on the lips.

"I'm going to shower and check on a few things. I'll be back later," he said.

I smiled. "I'm showering with you."

I couldn't get enough of him. After he left, I called Vanity and Crue to come over and join me and Drekia. I was going to put them to work. Everything needed to be in place before I called Jedrek to come home. I had approximately six hours before the sun started to set.

A Few Hours Later

"I need you to come home," I said calmly when Jedrek answered his.

"I'm coming," he replied before ending the call.

I smiled as I looked out onto the backyard. We did a great job with only six hours of time. Burgundy, crème, and mauve colored flowers decorated the backyard. All the chairs were positioned on each side of the off-white, long carpet. Judge Wilkins, a young, black, ambitious judge hoping to become president one day, stood under the beautifully decorated arch awaiting our presence. My only regret was I wished I had done this sooner.

"You better go get in that dress before he gets here," Drekia said excited. I giggled and rushed upstairs to get dressed.

My satin, off-white dress was nothing fancy. It had an open back, low cut front, three-inch straps and a small train. None of those things mattered to me anymore. I would marry Jedrek in one of his oversized T-shirts if I had to. Before slipping into my dress, Crue styled my curly tresses in a chic, messy bun. After slipping on my dress, Special did my makeup. I didn't know Special until Crue brought her over to my house after they had spent the day shopping together. Crue wasn't involved with Chike anymore, but she had developed a friendship with Special. She was determined to keep her drug free, and I admired her for doing that. Special talked about her love for doing make up before her drug habit. After she was done with my face, I slipped on my dress.

"You look so beautiful. Thank you for allowing me to be a part of this day," Special said giving me a warm embrace. She was a beautiful girl that had been through a hard time in life. I prayed she stayed on the right path.

"You're welcome."

Vanity walked into the room carrying my bouquet. "Yo future husband has arrived. He was having a panic attack until he saw the backyard. You should've seen him blushing. He's downstairs getting dressed."

"Thank y'all so much for making this happen for us," I said getting emotional.

"I can't believe my sister is getting married. Then again, I knew somebody would steal that heart," Vanity said. Tears started to fill our eyes.

"Nope! No crying!" Crue said. She passed each of us a glass of wine. Special declined because of her drug addiction. She didn't want to take the chance of becoming an alcoholic on top of her drug habit.

When I walked out to the backyard, I smiled at Jedrek. He was standing in front of the arch in his off-white and burgundy tuxedo. Yella Boy stood next to him in an off-white tuxedo. When I called Yella Boy, I didn't think he would be able to make it to the wedding, but he didn't hesitate to assure me that he would be here. Unfortunately, Zuri couldn't make it, but I understood with it being such short notice.

Drekia sat in the chair holding Lil J. Echon sat Blessing in his arms and EJ by his side. I was shocked to see Chike in attendance, but I was happy, nonetheless. Aunt Dee and her family were there. I had called Vonna to come to her only son's wedding, but she hadn't arrived yet. Since my dad couldn't be there, I had to walk down the aisle by myself. It was worth it seeing Jedrek waiting to be my husband. Luther Vandross' Here and Now started playing. I took a deep breath to hold in the tears before taking my walk down the aisle.

"Now, you didn't think I would miss this moment, did you?" Daddy's voice said behind me. I turned around to see my daddy standing tall and handsome in a black tuxedo. Mama was in a beautiful, long, white and burgundy two-piece dress and jacket.

"Daddy," I said throwing my arms around his neck. The flood gates opened, and I couldn't hold back the tears. Having my parents there made the moment an exceptional blessing.

"Your future husband looks like he's getting impatient," Daddy said blotting my face with a Kleenex.

After another tearful moment with Mama, she took her seat. Luther serenaded us again as we made our way down the aisle. Daddy kissed my cheeks telling me he loved me. He shook Jedrek's hand giving us his blessings. Jedrek stared at me with pure love and loyalty as my future husband, protector and lover. Vows weren't needed for us. We knew our love was forever. We couldn't fight it, even though we tried. Everyone sat quietly as Judge Wilkins commenced with the ceremony. It was time to place the rings on each other's fingers. I knew Jedrek didn't have a ring for me, and I understood. But he surprised me, when he turned to Yella Boy for the ring.

"I returned the other ring. I bought this one a couple of weeks ago," he said nervously. He was speaking of the spontaneous marriage he threw on me like I was doing to him. I giggled at how the tables had turned. I was overjoyed; he was more accepting of us getting married than I was at the time.

"I should've married you then," I said regretfully.

"We've been married since the first moment I met you," he said seriously. My heart melted.

"I now pronounce you man and wife. Do yo thang," Judge Wilkins said.

We all laughed. Jedrek pulled me into his arms for a long, passionate kiss while everyone applauded and cheered. I was now Mrs. Jedrek Jackson.

The rest of our evening was filled with partying, drinking and laughing. My heart didn't feel like every beat was a step closer to me leaving my family. My life felt like it was just beginning. This was what I wanted and needed. Daddy surprised us with a honeymoon trip, and the next morning, we were on our way to Switzerland to enjoy it like we didn't the first time we visited. Mama and Daddy agreed to keep Lil J, so we could enjoy our time as husband and wife.

Two Weeks Later

Quay

I finally found a decent apartment to move into. My next goal was to get a car. I was tired of catching Ubers everywhere I went. Crue wasted her money on expensive clothes and shoes and that was why she was still living in a hotel. I had always been smart with my finances. Chike thought Crue was the one he wanted to be with, but I knew he was wrong. She was going to do him like she did all the men that fell for her. Special was still staying at his house, and she had been drug free long enough to find her on way. He was probably back to fucking his baby mama. Maybe Chike would be the one to hurt Crue. I would love to see her hurting the way she hurt me.

I was sitting in the food court at the mall when I spotted Special. It surprised me because I didn't think she could come out alone. She appeared to be nervous as she looked around while talking on her phone. I immediately knew she was up to something and I wanted front row seats. I made sure she didn't see me as I followed her through the mall and then to the parking lot.

My knees buckled and my heart dropped when I saw who wrapped their arms around her. It was Khalil. So many questions started going through my mind. *How did she know him? Are they fucking or related? Is she trying to set Chike and Crue up for Khalil?*

I made sure not to be seen as they stood talking. One question was answered. They weren't any kin unless they were kissing cousins. After a hot kissing session, their conversation started to get heated. She jerked away from him and stormed back inside the mall. *What da fuck was that about?* Chike was dealing with two grimy bitches. *Karma comes quickly.* He should've treated me right. I was going to sit back and watch Special set them up. This show was getting better and better. I eased my way back inside the mall to find Special. She was walking inside the Cheesecake Factory. I waited to make sure she was alone before I approached her. She got a ticket from the hostess and took a seat in front; waiting for her number to be called.

"Hi," I said pretending to be shocked to run into her. She looked at me nervously.

"Hey. Quota or something right?" she asked. I knew the bitch was trying to be funny because Special knew my damn name.

"It's Quaysha," I replied dryly.

"Oh yea, sorry. Wasn't good with remembering names before the clean me," she said smiling. I forced a smile.

"Congratulations. I'm sure Chike is happy," I said.

"Not more than me. It feels good to be able to enjoy Krysta without that monkey on my back," she said. That lil brat would make anyone do drugs.

"I'm sure," I said nodding my head.

"Oh, that's my number for my table. It was nice seeing you," she said attempting to walk away.

"I'll join you. I was coming here to eat anyway," I said.

"Oh okay. I hate eating alone anyway. Someone was supposed to join me, but that didn't work out," she said.

"A date?" I asked as we walked to the table.

"Just someone I thought might be special, but you know how these niggas are," she said as we sat at our table.

"I thought you and Chike might try to work things out. You know, since you sober now. I'm sure your daughter would love to see you together," she said.

She laughed. "No, it's not like that with us anymore. Besides, I'm sure you know that already. He has this thing for Crue."

I couldn't reframe from rolling my eyes. "Yea, that was some low shit she did to me. We've been best friends for years; I would never sleep with a guy she liked."

"I can't speak on you and her situation. It's not my business. She's been a great supporter and friend to me," she said. Our waitress came and took our orders. After she left, I decided to build a wedge between her and Crue.

"Watch your back, because she doesn't like you. Only reason she's staying close to you is to make sure you stay away from Chike. She pretended to care for Krysta to get to him, and it worked. She's grimy, so be careful," I lied. I could see the concern fill her eyes. I planted the seeds needed. Special may be drug free, but her mind was still weak; I was sure of that.

"So, tell me about your friend," I said smiling. She looked sad.

"He's a nice guy, but he sells drugs and I can't have that in my life. He wants to come meet Chike, since I told him I live with my baby daddy. Chike demanded that I never bring anyone to his house, so he's mad I won't invite him over. I told him I can plan something at a restaurant for him to meet Chike," she said. This bitch was dumb. Khalil was using her to get to Chike, Crue and Jedrek.

"You met him on the streets?" I asked.

"No, I met him a month ago. I told him about my drug habit." she confessed.

"Chike can't choose who you spend your life with unless he's trying to make sure he still stands a chance with you," I said.

"I doubt it. He's just a private guy," she said.

"Well, don't end your new relationship to keep Chike happy. You deserve happiness too," I told her.

"Thank you for the advice." We made small talk as we ate lunch.

*****

I finally decided to answer Crue's phone call. She had been calling me for over a week, only to be sent to voicemail. I got enough information from Special to know Crue had cut Chike off. I was shocked when she told me to meet her at her new apartment. She nervously hugged me when she opened the door, but I didn't return the embrace. Just like mine, her apartment was nothing fancy, but hers was decorated beautifully with the furniture from Zelda's house.

"Thank you for coming," she said as we sat in her living room.

"You're welcome," I said dryly.

"Quaysha, I'm sorry. Everything I did was wrong. I knew it before and after it happened. We can never go back to the way things were, but I want to know you will one day forgive me," she said pitifully.

"You hurt me, Crue. You knew how I felt about him. You were intentionally telling me to fall back from him, so you could have him. Now, look at us. Neither one of us have him. He's living with his baby mama," I said.

I could see her mind wander off for just a moment. I wanted her to think Chike was fucking Special. Crue was a revengeful female when she felt like she was being played. She was going to be furious with Chike for causing her to lose her best friend, only for him to get back with Special. Even though she was playing it cool, I could see the hurt in her eyes. She was going to do something grimy to make sure he paid for hurting her. That would make him regret dealing with her.

"Chike's life isn't my concern. Our friendship is," she said.

"Why didn't you think about what this would do to our friendship before it happened?"

She dropped her head. "I thought it was a sexual attraction that would pass, but it didn't. I didn't lie to you about falling back from him so I could get close. I was only being honest. I tried staying away from him, but I couldn't. After our fight, nothing about being with him felt right."

"We can be friends again as long as you are done with him," I told her.

She looked at me with those fake ass tears in her eyes. "I really like him, Quay. Watching Zelda's life slowly slip from her made me realize life is too short. I'm not asking for your friendship or blessing. I know what I did is destroyed our friendship. I'm asking that you pray to make peace with what I did; not for me but for yourself. No, I'm not involved with him anymore, but I can't promise I never will be again. Right now, getting my life in order is my only concern."

This bitch! I screamed in my head. She calls me over here only to tell me some bullshit. I stood up and walked to the door. I turned back to face her.

"No wonder Quan was begging me for pussy all the time. He knew I was the better female unlike Chike. Don't think you're special to Chike. You just a hoe they passing around like a blunt. He'll never settle down with someone like you. Just remember you chose dick over your best friend," I said. I wanted her to feel those words.

Chike

I had been keeping myself busy, but nothing kept her off my mind. She barely looked at me at the wedding. Giving her space was getting harder every day. I broke down and popped up at the hotel, but she had checked out and quit her job. Realizing she was serious about ending things between us, I let her be…for now. Jedrek was still on his extended honeymoon and left me in charge. Money was coming in and everything was running smoothly until last night. Most of my time was spent in the streets or with Krysta. Special was still living with me, but we gave each other space.

I was sitting on the sofa putting on my shoes when Special walked out of her bedroom. Sometimes I wondered where we would be if she hadn't gotten addicted to drugs. She had life in her eyes now.

"Krysta finally talked herself to sleep," she said smiling. I loved watching her finally bond with Krysta. She sat next to me on the sofa.

"Yea, she's talked me to sleep many nights," I said laughing.

"Thank you, Chike. Thank you for being the best father for her. Thank you for not giving up on me. I will always be grateful for everything you have done for me, but it's time for me to face the world alone. You can't protect me from my habit forever. I know it'll be a fight every day, but I'm ready," she said.

"I understand. We can start looking for you a place tomorrow. We'll set up visits with Krysta for you," I said. I knew she was ready to move out. I'd heard her slipping out the house late at night sometimes. My heart wanted to stop her, thinking she was searching for drugs. But I knew I couldn't keep her caged in the house forever. It was a relief every time she returned drug free. She reached over and wrapped her arms around my neck. That was the first time we'd had any physical contact in a couple of years. Old memories started to cloud my judgment. The next thing I remember was her straddling my lap. Her wet tongue on my neck made my dick jump, but I wasn't thinking about her. My only thoughts were wishing she was Crue. I grabbed her around the waist and gently pushed her away.

"I'm so sorry," she said shamefully. Before I could respond, the front door slowly crept open. When I looked back over my shoulder, my heart dropped to the pit of my stomach. Crue stood there staring at us with solemn eyes.

"The door was unlocked," she said sadly before she rushed back out the door. I almost dropped Special on the floor trying to catch Crue before she left. Before I could make it outside, she was backing out of the driveway.

"Fuck!" I barked swinging at the air. Special was holding a piece of paper when I walked back inside.

"She was bringing this to you," she said holding out the paper. I took the paper that came from her notepad. There was a list of things she considered her flaws, and another list of the things she wanted to accomplish. Her accomplishments didn't state marrying a rich man. She wanted to marry a man that loved her regardless of her flaws. At the end of the lists was a note.

You made me see things in myself.

I wanted to share my flaws and goals with you.

Maybe we will meet again someday.

"I'll talk to her. We just got in the moment. I know there's nothing left between us," Special said. I prayed I didn't make the same mistake with her that I did with Quaysha.

"If I gave you that impression, I'm sorry. I'll always have love for you, but not in that way," I said.

She smiled. "You don't know your charisma. Shyma's gangsta ass raised a mean gentleman. I'll always have love for you also, but not in that way neither."

I walked over and flopped down on the sofa, reading Crue's list. She wanted to enroll in school to become a counselor for drug addicts. Her biggest flaw, not considering the consequences of her actions, was at the top of her list. All her flaws didn't matter to me anymore. I knew the person inside her. Special came and sat beside me.

"I'll make a deal with you," she said smiling.

"What?"

"Meet my friend, and I'll give you Crue's address," she said. I chuckled. Even though, she told me numerous times, she didn't know where Crue had moved.

"Who's your friend?" I asked. I was happy to see her moving on with her life, but I didn't think it was a good idea to be dating this soon. The happiness on her face made me decide to keep my opinion to myself.

"He's not from here. I like him a lot," she said blushing.

"Yea, we can do that," I said smiling at her.

"When?" she asked excited.

"You know the nigga ain't coming here. Set something up and let me know," I told her. No way was I letting a random nigga know where I lived.

"Okay," she said happily.

"I'm going to be spending most days at my shop working on some windows. I need you to stay with Krysta, because Ma's going on vacation," I told her, and she was overjoyed.

Two Months Later

Crue

I t had been two months since I caught Chike and Special together. I guess this was the karma Quay warned me about. My new job was the only thing keeping me from crying over him. My heart had always been guarded against men. He came and broke through the barriers, making me see the person I truly was. Whatever feelings I had for him, weren't reciprocated. Yet again, he proved I was always just sex. Quay's words kept ringing in my head as I cleaned up my station at the beauty salon. I had started a new job braiding hair, and I was making good enough money to afford my own apartment. The other hairdressers loved partying and chasing niggas with money. A few months ago, I would've gladly gone with them, but that girl wasn't me anymore. My focus was on making my own money and being happy.

They asked me to come out with them, but I declined. All I wanted was a shower and my bed. I loved my cozy, little apartment. Zelda gave me enough furniture to furnish every room. It was only a one bedroom, one bath, and small kitchen, and that was all I needed. The first thing I did was take a long, hot shower. Afterwards, Kevin Gates blasted through my surround sound. I rapped along with him while wrapped in a big towel and cooking teriyaki wings and fries.

I jumped when I heard the loud banging on my door. I walked over to the door, but I was too short to see through the peep hole.

"Who is it?" I asked nervously. Special, Vanity and Echon were the only ones that knew I stayed there, and they usually called before they came over. Vanity would send Echon over to survey my windows and doors to make sure no one had tried to break in. He was a weird acting guy, but cool. Zelda and Vanity had a thing for crazy men.

"Open the door," Chike demanded in a low voice.

My stomach fluttered. I never thought he would come to my apartment. I slowly removed all the locks. My heart pounded when I opened the door. His dark skin was beautiful with his fresh cut and trim. Like always, he never dressed up. The only time I'd seen him dressed for an occasion was at the wedding. I had to keep my eyes off him, because I wanted to fuck him on sight. He wore a pair of distressed jeans, a fitted black tee, and Van sneakers.

"You gon' let me in?" he asked. I snapped out of my trance and stepped to the side.

"I suppose you made Special tell you where I stay?" I asked.

"Nah, she volunteered the information. This nice. Zelda's furniture with a splash of Crue's flavor," he said sitting on the sofa looking around.

"Why are you here?" I asked with my hand on my hip. I was angry and hurt, but I wasn't going to let him see me weak. Men preyed on women's weakness.

"You know why I'm here," he said strolling through his phone.

He was acting nonchalant about me catching him with Special. I wasn't going to entertain him. I went back into the kitchen to finish my wings. I was glazing the wings with the teriyaki sauce when I felt his presence behind me. I wanted to turn around and slap the dog piss out of him, but I held my composure. At least I did until I felt his arm wrap around my waist. In one quick motion, I turned around and punched him in the face. He stumbled backwards, but I was the one in pain. I cried out placing my hand between my thighs. The pain was excruciating.

"Let me see," he said reaching for my hand.

"Stay the fuck away from me!" I screamed at him.

"It could be broke. Give me yo damn hand, Crue," he demanded calmly, reaching out for my hand. I slowly removed my hand from between my thighs. My entire hand was throbbing. Goose bumps popped on my body when I placed my hand in his.

"Move your fingers," he said looking at my hand. It hurt to move them, but they moved.

"They're not broken. Probably just jammed it when you hit me. It's going to swell and ach for a few days," he said.

"Great! Now I can't do hair until the swelling goes down. I have to cancel all my appointments for the next few days! Thanks a-damn-lot!" I said angrily.

"I ain't tell yo ass to be Mike Tyson," he said. I rolled my eyes at him. He started gently massaging my fingers. I snatched my hand away from him when my pussy throbbed from his touch.

"Fine Chike! You come here to fuck me and go back home. Here! That's all I'm worth anyway right?" I asked snatching my towel from around me and jumping up on the counter. I spread my legs and invited him to take what he came for. I could see his dick hardening. He grabbed me around the waist and stood me on the kitchen floor, wrapping my towel around me.

"I came to apologize for what you saw. We were having an emotional moment and took it to a place neither of us want. Special is somebody important in my life, because we share a child together. The only thing I could think about was what it would feel like to have you riding my dick," he said with a straight face.

"I just offered to fuck you," I said still mad with him.

"I didn't come here for that. You dropped this," he said showing me the list I had come to bring him before saying goodbye.

"You keep it," I said attempting to walk away. He grabbed me by my waist.

"I accept you flaws and all," he whispered in my ear. I turned around to face him. He was what I wanted, but I also needed to grow on my own.

"I have a lot of growing to do. I don't wanna mess this up by making rash decisions. Can we please slow this down? Like you take me on dates and romantic walks?" I said smiling.

He laughed. "What kind of rash decisions?"

"After walking in on you and Special, I was considering fucking you and robbing that built in safe behind you and Krysta's picture," I said smiling. He laughed hysterically.

"You gotta be more creative," I told him and laughed with him.

"Now finish cooking. I'm hungry," he said tapping me on the ass.

"Nigga, you don't pay no bills here to be giving orders. I'm the boss here," I said proudly.

My small apartment was the first thing I'd owned without using men. I got it from working hard. He pulled me into his chest and slid his hand between my thighs. I was embarrassed by him discovering my soaked pussy.

"I can eat you or the wings. You choose," he said licking his lips.

My juices slid between my thighs thinking about his tongue tasting me, but I chose the wings. I wanted to spend

time building our friendship and hopefully relationship.
Chike was nothing like the man I imagined building a life
with. He wasn't rich and successful. That was all I ever
wanted in a man until I met him. He was smart, ambitious
and a great father. He also thought I was worth his time.
After I was done with the wings and fries, we sat in the
living room eating. My feet were relaxed on his lap.

"Ewww," I sighed when he stuck my toes in his plate
smearing them with teriyaki sauce. I bit my bottom lip
when he slowly started licking the sauce from my toes.
After he cleaned my toes, he stood up.

"I gotta go check up on the corners," he said. He
leaned down and kissed me on the forehead. I threw one of
my throw pillows at his back.

"That was wrong!" I yelled at him. He laughed at
leaving me dripping wet. When he opened my door,
Special was standing on the other side getting ready to
knock. He looked back at me to make sure to let her in. I
shrugged my shoulders.

"Shyma came to pick Krysta up. She wants to keep her
tonight, since she'll be gone for a week. Hope that was
okay," she said to Chike.

"Yea, that's a'ight," he said. Special walked in as he walked out. I sat up on the sofa to let her sit on the opposite end. She didn't hesitate to start talking, so I listened.

"That was the first time something like that ever happened between us. He really likes you and I do too. I'm not trying to get back in Chike's life that way. I'm so appreciative of him for not giving up on me when my own family turned their backs on me. He's given me a chance to make my life meaningful. I was a walking zombie. I'll always have love for him for doing that. Did you know he fought my parents for custody of Krysta?"

"He did?" I asked surprised.

"Yea. He won but gave them visitation voluntarily. My parents are loaded. They only wanted Krysta as a possession and victory trophy. Daddy hates to lose. Ever since they lost the custody battle, they hardly come to get her. The only spend time with her when it's convenient for them. I was the perfect daughter to show off until I found drugs as a relief from being ignored by them. I know most people don't think being rich comes with many problems, but it does. I never felt loved or wanted by my parents. They only had a child to complete their picture-perfect lives. When the drugs took me over, they didn't think twice about disowning me. They couldn't let me ruin their perfect image."

"I'm sorry," I said honestly.

"I want you to be in Krysta's life if I'm not strong enough to stay clean. Some days the urge to take a hit is too much," she said.

"You're going to stay clean, Special. We're going to make sure that happens. What do you want to do with your life now?" I assured her.

She shrugged her shoulders. "I don't know. I just want to do something that I can be proud of."

"Taking it day by day is something you should be extremely proud of," I told her.

She smiled at me. "Thank you for being a good friend."

I hugged her. "You're welcome."

"Oh yea, I ran into Quay. She's still pissed with you. She was telling me stuff about you to turn me against you. I don't get involved with best friend drama, so I kept my mouth shut and listened."

"What did she say?" I asked curiously.

SOUL Publications

"That you didn't like me, and you were faking your love for Krysta to get to Chike," Special informed me. I knew Quay was furious with me, but I never thought she would lie on me.

"I would never fake love for a child, Special. I don't even know if that's possible. And my friendship to you is genuine. There's no reason for me to pretend to like you," I assured her.

She smiled. "I know. She's just still hurt and angry."

I laughed. "Did she tell you she was fucking Quan while he was my so-called boyfriend?"

Special's eyes grew big before we burst out laughing. I wished things could've been this way between me and Quaysha. I often wondered how she was doing. She had always been smart and determined. Maybe being away from me would help her to become her own woman. Quaysha always felt like she was in my shadow, and I felt like I needed her to be by my side. Sometimes, people needed to grow a part to find themselves.

Special ended up crashing on my sofa. The next morning, I cooked us breakfast. My hand was swollen and aching, and I had to call to cancel or reschedule my appointments. I was ecstatic when everyone agreed to reschedule. There was no point in showing up if I couldn't do hair. I sat on the sofa eating my grits, eggs and bacon. Special was on the sofa giggling as I cooked us breakfast. She finally joined me with her plate of food.

"So, fill me in on the man that's got you smiling like that," I said.

She blushed. "He's tall, dark and handsome with the cleanest long dreads."

"Let me see. I know you got some pictures in your phone," I said. She smiled and started strolling through her phone. My heart dropped and I jumped up from the sofa; my plate of food landed on my hardwood floor.

"What? What's wrong?" Special asked me.

Water filled my eyes. "Special this is the guy that shot Zelda. It's the one I robbed. He wants to kill Jedrek, and probably Chike," I said with a trembling voice. Special's mouth dropped open.

"Come on! We have to tell Chike and Jedrek," I said hurrying to my bedroom to put on some clothes.

"Crue, he's going to see Chike right now," Special hollered as I rushed in the bedroom. I stopped and faced her.

"What? Why?" I asked.

"Chike had sent me a text earlier to pick Krysta up from the workshop, because Shyma had dropped her off this morning. He took her with him. Kwame had been pressing me about meeting Chike, so I gave him the address to the workshop," she said with tears falling down her face.

"Oh my God," I said softly thinking the worst.

"We have to go out there. He doesn't have service that far in the woods for me to call his phone," she said hysterically.

"I'm going to call Jedrek," I said. I called Jedrek's number, but he didn't answer. Calling Zelda wasn't an option, so I called Echon. He ended the call without replying to what Special had revealed.

"I can't stay here and wait. My baby is out there!" Special said grabbing her car keys.

"No! What are you going to do?" I said grabbing her wrist. I held her so tight, my swollen hand ached.

"I have a gun that Chike always made me carry for protection. Don't you have one?" Special asked me.

"Yea, but I barely know how to use it. Echon is going out there and I'm sure Jedrek is armed. You know as well as I do Chike has an armory out there. We will only be a distraction," I tried convincing her.

She finally tried to relax, but I could see she was panicking. We both needed a blunt right now, but neither of us smoked. My heart was racing as I kept calling Chike's phone. I was only in the bedroom a couple of minutes, and those couple of minutes gave Special the opportunity to escape. I rushed out the apartment to stop her, but she was pulling off in her car. I hurried back inside and grabbed my keys. Calling the cops wasn't an option. Chike had too many guns out there. I prayed as I hopped in my car and tried to catch up with Special.

Earlier

Zelda

Our honeymoon was everything I wanted and more. We didn't want to come back, but we missed our son. Being back home reminded me that my heart was weakening every day. Some days I could barely pull myself out of bed, so Jedrek made sure someone was always with me. I prayed every night for God to bless me with a new heart, because I wasn't ready to leave my family.

Jedrek walked in the bedroom interrupting my thoughts. His body was pouring in sweat due to the vigorous workouts he used to relieve stress. Normally he would use my body for his workout, but I was too weak for us to have sex. I wasn't one of those women that would understand if her husband fucked another female, because she wasn't able. I'd cut his dick off if he stuck it in another woman. The thought of that possibility made my heart race.

Jedrek had a lot going on, but he wouldn't tell me. He didn't want me stressing about anything. I slowly sat up in the bed and called him over. He sat on the end of the bed.

"Maybe I'm supposed to tell you to find sex elsewhere, since I'm unable. But I'll cut it off before I say those words," I said with a smile.

He laughed. "When you get the new heart, I'm putting every muscle to work."

"I want you to leave the streets alone," I told him.

"I'm making that happened now. I don't want Chike taking over. He has a daughter he needs to raise. I'm trying to honor his request and let Quan step up," he said.

"How's that working out?" I smiled. He wasn't a big fan of Quan's.

"Surprisingly well. I'm getting his head in the game. I don't want to throw him all this money and power with no knowledge," he informed me.

"That's good," I said.

"I went by to visit Crue like you requested. I made peace with her. No more animosity. She can be over-damn-dramatic just like you," he said smiling. I laughed, because it was the truth. I saw so much of my younger self in Crue.

"Thank you so much for doing that," I said graciously.

"I almost choked her to death, because she wouldn't stop apologizing and crying. Only thing that saved her was Chike coming inside the apartment," he said. He may have been joking, but I knew he wanted to kill someone. He had a lot of rage inside of him because of what happened to me. I knew it took a lot for him to forgive Crue.

"Sorry to interrupt, but you have a visitor," Drekia said sticking her head in the door.

"Who is it?" Jedrek asked protectively.

"Quay," Drekia said.

"You feel like company?" Jedrek asked me.

"Yea, I've been waiting for her to come see me," I assured him. He told me he was going to Chike's workshop to discuss some business with him. Jedrek had plans to invest in Chike's business.

"Well, I'm going to have lunch with the mother from *Mommy Dearest* at Zelda's request," Drekia said rolling her eyes at me jokingly. I laughed. I wanted to see her, Jedrek and Vonna heal their relationship before I left this earth.

"Vonna didn't beat you," Jedrek said.

"Still doesn't mean she's not Mommy Dearest," Drekia said smiling and winking her eye before she left the room.

"Let me shower and shit before you send her up," Jedrek yelled at Drekia.

"Gotcha," Drekia yelled back.

"The nurse is here if you need help with Lil J," he said before hopping in the shower.

A half an hour later, Quay walked in my bedroom. She looked beautiful as always, but she held a confidence about herself that I'd never seen. We gave each other a warm hug, before she sat on the edge of the bed. She took Lil J from my arms and played with him until he started to whine. The nurse took him downstairs to feed him. He was getting so big, so quick.

We talked about fashion, makeup and other irrelevant topics. I told her to treat me like this was another day at my house having girl talk and not like I was dying. I listened as she filled me in on what was going on in her life. She was still working her two jobs and going to school to become a nurse. Her ultimate goal was to own her own hospice business. She never mentioned Crue, so I decided to bring her into the conversation.

"And how are things with Crue?" I asked. She shocked me and started crying uncontrollably. Her soft cries of apologies left me confused. I held her until she stopped crying not understanding what she was apologizing for.

"I didn't mean for things to go this way. I only wanted to pay Crue back for messing with Chike," she said looking at me with pleading eyes.

"What did you do, Quay?" I asked. I sat in shock listening to her tell me how she set up the fake kidnapping and gave Khalil the code to my house.

"Why would you do that, Quay?" I asked getting emotional.

"I wanted him, and she made him fall for her. He needed to know the type of person she was. I never planned on you getting shot. You weren't supposed to be there. I'm so sorry, Zelda," she said crying again. For the first time in months, I was angry.

"You can't blame Crue for Chike's feelings for her. Yes, she was dead ass wrong for taking it there with him knowing how you felt. Quay, you knew it was happening, but you chose to play the victim with them. You tried playing on their emotions and it backfired. You thought Crue would do whatever to make you happy, but this time it didn't work. This is no different than you claiming to be recorded having sex without your consent." Her eyes bulged out her head.

"Yea, I know you wanted to be recorded. Mama was and still is good friends with the young man you had sex with. Since you and Crue have been here, I've observed your friendship. You are the victim and she is the savior, but Crue chose her heart over you this time. You must stop playing the victim just like Crue must admit to her wrong doings. I will take this information to my grave, because it isn't my truth to tell. You haven't been innocent in any of this. It's not fair that you have left Crue to carry all the guilt."

She double shocked me by telling me that Special was dating the guy that shot me. I tried to remain calm, but I was losing my cool with her. Quay had stood by for months and let everyone's life be in jeopardy for her selfish revenge.

"You better pray nothing happens to any of them. Their blood will be on your hands," I warned her.

I was furious with her, but she needed guidance. Turning her away wasn't going to help her. I sat and talked with her about growing up and stepping out of Crue's shadow. Vanity walked into the bedroom holding Blessing and sat on the opposite side of the bed with me. She had left EJ downstairs with the nurse playing with Lil J.

"What brings you over?" I asked. The look in her eyes told me something was wrong, but she was trying to stay calm for me. She stared me in the eyes.

"When Echon leaves the house without saying a word, I worry. Coming to see you and my godson keeps me from stressing too much," she said. My gut told me something was wrong.

Jedrek

Everything happened so fast. I walked out of Chike's workshop to get a blunt from my car and bullets started flying everywhere. We were caught off guard by the shots coming from the bushes. Chike rushed out throwing me a nine-millimeter. We fired toward the bushes, shielding behind Chike's truck, but the bullets were still coming. Our nines were no competition for the automatic firing at us.

"Cover me! I'm going to get two automatics!" Chike yelled at me passing me his gun.

Seconds later, he rushed back outside passing me an AK-47. We looked at each other when we heard Special and Crue's voices. Special was calling Krysta's name while Crue begged her to stop running in our direction. Khalil stepped out the bushes blazing bullets toward us. We had to take Khalil out before he killed them. Krysta must've heard her mother's voice and took off running out the workshop. We rushed behind Krysta with the automatics in our hands trying to protect her small body. Our bullets were able to knock Khalil to the ground, but not take him out. He had to be wearing a vest. I know we hit him a few times in the chest area. We were too focused on protecting Krysta and

Special to focus on shooting him in the head. Echon stepped from the bushes and put two holes in his head. The gunshots stopped, but all we could hear was horrifying screams coming from Crue. Special was bleeding from the head as she lay on top of Krysta's body. Chike rushed over and rolled Special off Krysta. Krysta cried quietly with fear engraved in her eyes.

"She gotta pulse," Chike said scooping Special into his arm.

"I need you to calm the fuck down, and take my daughter to my house," he said to Crue. She stopped crying and nodded her head.

"Put her in my car," I told Chike because his truck was covered with bullet holes. I drove Chike and Special to the hospital, and Echon followed Crue back to Chike's house. I knew Echon would call a clean-up crew for Khalil's body.

Chike

Jedrek instructed me what and what not to say to the cops. I couldn't concentrate on their questions because I was thinking about Special. None of this made sense. *How did Khalil know about the workshop? What was Special and Crue doing there?* Those two questions kept ringing in my head. I sat in the waiting room praying Special pulled through. Jedrek walked over to me after talking to the cops and sat next to me.

"They're going to notify her parents," he told me.

All I did was shake my head. This wasn't going to go well with them. They hated everything about me and blamed me for Special's drug addiction. It only got worse when I won custody of Krysta. But this time it was my fault. She wouldn't be lying in there with a bullet in her head if it wasn't for my beef with Khalil. A flood of emotions ran through my body. Anger was the one that took control.

"I have to go get Krysta," I said standing.

"Woah! She's seen enough. She's safe with Crue. I've already sent someone to watch your house. Just in case

Khalil wasn't working alone," he said. I ignored him and walked away.

*****

"Krysta," I said calling her name when I walked in my house. I knew they were there because Crue's car was parked in the driveway. I opened Krysta's bedroom door. She was wrapped in Crue's arms, asleep. Crue put her finger to her lips motioning for me to be quiet. I walked into the kitchen, grabbing a bottle of Hennessey and chugged from the bottle. Crue walked into the kitchen with blood shot eyes.

"Please tell me she's going to be okay," she said as tears started to fall down her eyes.

"Get da fuck out of my house! You brought that nigga into all of lives," I spewed at her. It crushed me to see the look of hurt covering her face. I regretted hurting her, but I didn't regret what I felt. She stood before me crying uncontrollably as her body trembled. I was furious and couldn't console her, so I walked away and into Krysta's bedroom. I sat on the edge of the bed watching my baby girl sleep peaceful. When she woke up, her dreams would turn into the nightmare she had witnessed today. I pulled out my phone and called Ma. She answered on the second ring.

"Ma," I said trying to hold back tears.

"What's wrong, baby?" she said worriedly.

"I need to bring Krysta to you," I said.

"Bring her now. We'll talk," she said ending the call. Ma knew something bad had happened. When the streets had a hold on me, she never gave up on me. It was like I had a death wish, doing shit that could've had me in a body bag. She fought me with everything she had to save me from ending up dead or in prison for life. That was why I couldn't give up on Special. It was my turn to give back what Ma gave to me, giving someone another chance at a meaningful life. When I walked out the bedroom, with Krysta in my arms, Crue was gone.

*****

When I walked in Ma's house, she was in the kitchen cooking. I took Krysta to her bedroom and laid her in the bed. I was relieved that she was still asleep. I went into the kitchen and sat at the table. Ma sat across from me.

"What happened?" she asked. She sat quietly listening to me tell her everything that happened at the workshop. Ma wasn't the suburban type of mom, so she wasn't surprised by what happened. She'd lived the street life before she gave birth to me.

"Is she?" she asked.

"I don't know. I left the hospital to get Krysta," I explained.

"Wait a minute. Where was Krysta? I thought you said she was there."

"She was, but I sent her to my house with Crue," I told her.

"So, where's Crue?" she asked. I took a deep breath and ran my hand over my face. When I told her what I did to Crue, her concerned face turned into a scowl.

"You dead ass wrong, Chike," she said calmly staring at me.

"I feel that now. I was in my damn feelings at the time. I need to get back to the hospital. Krysta gon' be fucked up when she wakes up. She saw everything, Ma."

"I got her. Go," she said standing up. I stood up with her.

"Thank you," I said. We shared a tight hug before I left.

*****

When I returned to the hospital, Special's parents were sitting in the waiting room. Her father gave me the look of death. Jedrek was sitting in a corner on his cellphone. Crue was sitting by herself, with her head down, across from Special's parents. I took a deep breath and walked over to Special's parents. Her father stood up, standing just as tall as me at six-foot two inches with his brown skin complexion and clean shaven face. He was a slender man with low afro. Special's mom was a mixture of black, white and Honduran. She was medium height with long, straight hair, and a

"Please just get him out of here. I don't want him anywhere near my child," Mrs. Clayton, Special's mother cried.

"It's best you leave. You have done enough for our daughter," Special's dad said. I chuckled in his face and walked away. His perception of me wasn't my concern. I walked over and stood in front of Crue.

"I need to talk to you in the hall," I said calmly. She rolled her eyes at me and walked away. Jedrek walked up to me.

"Zelda's freaking out. I need to check on her. Hit me up if you need anything…I mean anything," he said glancing over my shoulder at Special's parents. A word from me and they would both be dead.

"They ain't no threat," I assured him. He dapped me up before walking out of the waiting room.

When I walked into the hallway, Crue was leaning against the wall with her arms folded across her waist. I leaned against the opposite wall. Her eyes were swollen and red from crying. All I wanted to do was hold her.

"Why did you and Special come to the workshop?" I asked.

"She slipped away from me when I went into my bedroom. I tried following her to stop her from coming there?" she explained.

"And why was she coming there?" I asked.

"She's been involved with him for a while. I never even knew she was seeing someone. This morning she finally told me and showed me his picture. She had told him he was working at your workshop and gave him the address. I told her who he was, and she panicked. All she could think about was protecting Krysta," she said. She started crying softly and walked away from me. I grabbed her by the arm.

"I'm sorry for what I said. I was in a fucked up place," I said.

"No apologies needed. You spoke the truth," she said gently pulling away from me.

She went back into the waiting room. I wanted to stay away from Special's parents, so I sat on the floor in the hall. It took hours for a tall, white doctor to come update us on Special's condition. I followed him into the waiting room, and everyone anxiously stood up. The doctor introduced himself as Dr. Melbourne.

"How's my daughter?" Mrs. Clayton asked. The doctor went into a long speech about Special's injuries.

"Will she pull through?" Mr. Clayton asked.

"Unfortunately, the chances are very slim. Your daughter has no brain activity," Dr. Melbourne stated. I closed my eyes to hold the tears. Crue fell to the floor crying. Mrs. Clayton fainted, but her husband caught her before she hit the floor.

"I know this is traumatic for your family. I will give you time to decide," Dr. Melbourne said.

"There's nothing to decide. Our daughter will pull out of this. We will not be taking her from the machines," Mr. Clayton stated.

"I will give you time," Dr. Melbourne stated before walking out the room. I followed him.

"Doc," I said getting his attention. He turned to face me.

"Is there a chance she could pull through this?" I asked. He didn't have to speak. His facial expression said it all.

"I don't want this hoodlum and his friends near my child. If they are, I will have them arrested and sue this damn hospital!" Mr. Clayton raged walking into the hallway. I had heard enough of him. I walked toward him, ready to lay him on the floor.

"Chike!" Crue shouted. I stopped and stared at her.

"That's what he wants. Let's just leave," she said calmly.

"I ain't leaving her here with these mothafuckas. They don't give a damn about her!" I barked staring at her father. Crue walked up and stood between me and Mr. Clayton.

"Please. Krysta needs you right now," she pleaded with me. All the rage shifted from my body thinking about my daughter. Me and Ma was all she had now.

Six Months Later

Crue

My life consisted of work, school, visiting the hospital and staying home. If someone had told me this would be my life a year ago, I would've never believed it. When I wasn't at work or school, I spent my time at the hospital with Zelda. My heart shattered every time I visited her. She had tried to be strong for so long, but her weak heart was winning the battle. She was confined to the hospital, and I hated feeling like we were sitting around waiting for her to die. Most of the time, she barely knew we were there, but Jedrek wouldn't leave her side. Her parents had practically moved here to help with Lil J.

Zelda made Jedrek promise he wouldn't put a heart inside her body without knowing who it belonged to. He battled with that promise every day. In the past two months, he'd had several altercations with her parents and Vanity about honoring her wish.

Special's parents still had her own life support even though they knew there was no chance of her waking up. I couldn't understand it. All of us were still barred from seeing Special, but I had my ways of getting around that. I slipped into her room late at night when I knew her parents weren't going to pop up. They hardly showed up in the daytime either. Tonight, I sat by her bed still amazed at what I was seeing. This was the reason they wanted to keep her alive. They wanted a second chance at being parents. Special's belly had grown tremendously over the last six months. She was two months pregnant when she was shot, making her eight months pregnant now.

"Hi Special. I know you can't hear me, but this little beautiful life inside of you can. I don't' know how, but I'm going to be a part of its life. I'm so glad I got the chance to meet and become your friend," I said touching her belly. Her room door slowly opened, and my heart dropped, thinking I had been caught. It was Chike. The butterflies in my stomach fluttered and my heart pounded. I hadn't seen him since the day we walked out the hospital together. I dropped him off at his mother's, and we never said a word to each other. I had missed him so much, but I knew I was a reminder of what happened to Special.

"I'm sorry. I'll leave," I said walking toward the door. He wrapped his arm around my waist when I tried to walk past him. Tingling sensations flowed through my body from his touch.

"You don't have to leave," he said.

"Thank you," I said softly, looking up at him. His eyes were focused on Special. He released me and walked over to her bed.

"I sneak in here. I wanted to kill them for keeping her alive this way until I found out she was pregnant. She's carrying the nigga's baby that killed her," he said looking at her belly.

"Do you think she would want it?" I asked walking over and standing beside him.

"I don't know if she would've kept it, but she definitely would've had it. She didn't believe in abortion even in rape or incest," he said.

"Do they bring Krysta to see her?" I asked. I had thought about his beautiful daughter as much as I'd thought of him.

"Yea, the seven times they've been to see her. They call the doctor regularly to check on the progress of her pregnancy. I bring Krysta with me sometimes," he said. He applied some lip balm to her dry lips. We sat by her bedside watching her sleep. The night nurses were familiar with both of us, so they allowed us to stay.

"How's your mom and Krysta" I asked.

"They're good. She still asks about you," he said glancing at me.

I smiled happy that she remembered me. "Tell her I said hi."

He stared at me this time. "You can tell her yourself. I don't have a problem, with you visiting them some time. I have to get Krysta, because Ma gotta be at work in a couple of hours," he said standing up. He kissed Special on the forehead and gave me his attention.

"How's school?" he asked. I didn't know he knew I was enrolled in school.

I smiled. "It's a challenge, but I'm handling it." He leaned down and kissed my lips softly. I wanted to ravish him, but I contained myself. He left me sitting there stuck.

I stayed with Special so long, I fell asleep. When I woke up, I hurried out of the room before the wrong person saw me. Since I was already at the hospital, I decided to visit Zelda before going home. Luckily for me, it was Sunday which meant no school or work. When the elevator doors opened on Zelda's floor, my heart felt like it stopped. Vanity and Aunt Crystal were crying uncontrollably, and Uncle Tony and Echon were holding on to Jedrek.

"Please don't leave me! Zelly baby! Please! I'm begging you!" Jedrek cried out as they tried to pull him out of the room. When they got him all the way out of the room, he pushed them away. He fell to his knees and cried like a baby. Seeing him broken like this was too much for anyone to witness. Doctors and nurses rushed past me and into the room. I couldn't stop my tears as we all stood outside her room crying like babies. A few minutes passed, before Dr. Bailon walked out of the room.

"Mr. Jackson," Dr. Bailon said as he walked out of the room. Jedrek wouldn't look up at him as he stayed kneeled on the floor. Dr. Bailon pulled her face mask from his mouth and kneeled to speak to him.

"She's still with us," he said placing his hand on Jedrek's shoulder. Jedrek fell back against the wall and watched Dr. Bailon walk back into the room. When he was out of our sight, Jedrek stood up and walked over to Echon.

"Get the heart. I don't give a fuck who it belonged to," he said. He didn't give anyone a chance to reply before walking into the room with his wife. This would destroy their marriage if she survived.

Two Days Later

Chike

Sleep was a stranger to me. My life was dedicated to my daughter. She had nightmares for months after the shooting, but slowly, Krysta was finally becoming herself. If I wasn't spending time with Krysta, my mind was on Special. I hated that her parents would get custody of her child. They were going to use her baby to eliminate the guilt they felt for throwing their daughter to the streets. Many nights I had to pray to keep from ending their lives. Other times, my heart was missing Crue.

"Boy, just call the girl," Ma said.

"What you talking about?" I said sitting up on the sofa.

"You over there falling asleep and mumbling that child's name," she said.

I chuckled, because she wasn't lying. Many nights I'd caught myself calling her name in my sleep. Seeing her at the hospital the other night made me miss her more. Crue wasn't to blame for Special getting shot, but I stayed away from her so long, because I knew my words hurt her. An apology couldn't fix what I said to her. We needed time apart to grieve for Special.

"Well, ain't this some shit. Look who coming to my door," she said smiling at me. She passed me her cellphone and I saw Crue walking up to Ma's front door. I jumped up and rushed to open the door. Something had to be wrong to bring her here.

"What's wrong?" I asked opening the door.

"You may kill me for asking this, but I have to try," she said. I moved to the side and let her come in. Krysta ran to her calling out her name. When she reached her, she wrapped her little arms around Crue's legs. Crue picked her up and gave her a tight hug.

"Come on, Krysta. Let's go in your room and play. Daddy needs to talk to his long, lost girlfriend," Shyma said standing up as Crue put Krysta down.

"I would like to speak with you also. Plus, you may have to save my life from Chike after he hears what I have to say," she said nervously. *She better not tell me she knew Special was fucking Khalil*, I thought to myself and immediately started to get angry.

"Krysta, I'll be there in a minute," Shyma yelled. She invited Crue to have a seat in the den, and I sat in the recliner. Ma and Crue sat on opposite ends of the couch. She proceeded to tell us her reason for coming here. I didn't know how to feel about what she had said, but I felt like it would serve a purpose.

Ma looked at me and shrugged her shoulders. "It's worth a try."

"Let's go," I said to Crue.

*****

"I thought you would kill me when I told you my idea," Crue said as I drove.

"I would never hurt you," I told her. We pulled in front of a huge white mansion. I hated the plantation style mansions.

"Stay here. They might shoot on sight when they see me at the door," I said seriously.

She opened the door. "No, I'm coming with you."

I smiled at her. "You willing to risk yo life for a nigga?"

"Every day," she said. We got out of the truck, and she walked to my side of the truck.

"I like the new truck," she said smiling at me.

"Same truck. Different color," I said taking her hand.

We walked up the stairs and rang the doorbell. After the third ring, an elderly black lady finally opened the door. Surprisingly, she stepped to the side to invite us in and instructed us to follow her. I guess they saw us arriving at their home on the security monitor. We followed her down a long hall. Mr. Clayton was sitting behind a tall, tarnished, cedar oak desk. The study was enormous and cold. A huge picture of him and his wife hung over his head against the wall. My only thoughts were that Special wasn't in the photo.

"I'm feeling generous today. You have five minutes, before you are escorted off my property. So, speak," he said.

"May I sit?" Crue asked nicely. He nodded his head for her to take a seat in front of his desk. Crue sat and looked back at me, gesturing for me to take a seat beside her. I reluctantly sat next to her.

"Mr. Clayton, thank you so much for inviting us into your beautiful home. This could be a very brief conversation, but I'm hoping what I have to say will allow us to discuss things further," Crue said to him. She was polite and smooth. He nodded his head for her to continue.

"I grew up with a father that was addicted to crack, and he still is. I resented my mother for not walking away from him, because I didn't understand what it was like to love someone so much. I vowed never to love anyone that way, so I used men for what I could get from them. Moving to Atlanta with my cousin, Zelda, changed my way of thinking. She has a successful career as a prominent lawyer, a devoted husband, and a handsome baby boy. Zelda was shot by the same man that shot Special. Seeing the kind of love Zelda and Jedrek had for each other changed me slowly.

"I met Special through Chike. I know you have resentment toward him, but he's the most loving father to your granddaughter, and he never gave up on Special. Special wanted to get better and she did. She was drug free for months before she was shot, and during that time we became very good friends. I spent many days helping her stay clean, and what I learned was that she wanted a meaningful life. Laying there isn't the way she would want her life to be.

My cousin's heart was severely damaged when she was shot. I'm pleading with you with all I have inside me to save my cousin's life. I'm begging you to give her a chance to live a life making beautiful memories with her family. Special is an organ donor. Let go of the hate you have for Chike and let Special's life serve its purpose," Crue said as tears flowed down her face.

"Zelda Vandross is your cousin?" Mrs. Clayton asked walking in the room, standing next to her husband.

"Yes ma'am. Our mothers are sisters," Crue said to her. Mr. and Mrs. Clayton looked at each other, before Mrs. Clayton gave me her attention.

"You led our daughter down this road. She wouldn't stay away from your," she said angrily to Chike.

"Your daughter couldn't stay away from the drugs. You pushed her to the streets by not giving her the love and attention she needed. I've been sitting around this big ass room looking at all the family pictures. Twenty pictures, and Special is only in two of them. And those were charity events where you used her to create the perfect family image and collect money. I loved your daughter and I'm sorry for what has happened to her, but I will not let you blame me for it."

I stood up to leave. They would never give us Special's heart. Crue could cry blood and they still wouldn't do it because of their hate for me.

"Sit down," Mr. Clayton said loudly as I walked away. I stopped and turned to face them, but he was looking at Crue.

"Ms. Vandross was my brother-in-law's lawyer. It was one of the most high-profile cases in Atlanta, and she was able to get all the charges dropped," he said.

Crue smiled. "Her last name is Jackson now."

"How do we even know if she is a match for Special's heart?" Mrs. Clayton asked.

"Two nights ago, I watched her husband break down in a way that I didn't think was possible because Zelda slipped away from us for a few minutes. I pleaded with Special's doctor and Zelda's doctors to see if they matched. The results aren't back yet, but if they are, we will need your consent to remove Special from life support," Crue explained.

"I can have both doctors' licenses taken for what they did," Mr. Clayton said.

"You'll be dead first," I warned him. I heard a gasp come from Mrs. Clayton.

Mr. Clayton stood up. "Leave now. We need time to discuss this."

"Thank you so much for your time," Crue said standing up. Crue didn't say a word to me until we got in the truck.

"Da fuck was that?" she asked, slapping me in the back of my head.

"What?" I asked shocked by her outburst.

"Threatening to kill him in our time of need," she said angrily. I shrugged my shoulders.

"What now?" I asked.

"We wait for the results. Are you okay with this, if she's a match?" she asked nervously.

"I think it would make Special happy to know her heart will be loved my Zelda," I told her, and she smiled.

*****

When we got back to the house, Ma and Krysta were gone. I called her phone and found out she took Krysta out for ice cream. Crue wanted to spend some time with her and style her hair before she left; plus, I didn't want her to leave, so I told her they would be back shortly.

I had been working at my workshop earlier, so I went to get in the shower and Crue waited on the couch. As I was in the shower, my dick got brick hard thinking about her thick thighs. I stepped out the shower and wrapped a towel around me. I called Ma and told her to take Krysta to my house after their ice cream date. Once that was settled, I walked into the den where Crue was sitting up on the sofa asleep. She jumped when she felt my presence.

"Sorry, I haven't slept much," she said.

"You good," I said smiling down at her.

She became fully awake, and noticed I was only wearing a towel. Crue playfully yanked at the towel making it fall to the floor. Her eyes were glued to my stiff dick as she wrapped her soft hand around my shaft. She looked up at me as she massaged me. I fought against the groan that wanted to be set free but lost when her wet tongue licked my dome and my dick jumped in her hand. Her eyes stayed on me as she lubricated my dome and massaged my shaft.

She started licking up and down my shaft, moaning as she made my dick sloppy wet.

Crue took me inside her mouth, draping her lips around my shaft. Her eyes stayed focused on mine as she sucked me in and out of her mouth. My dome was tapping against her throat. Pulling me out of her mouth, she beat my dick with her hands. She smiled up at me with glazed lips and saliva dripping from her chin. She continued to knead my shaft and started caressing my balls until pre-cum oozed from my dome.

"Fuck!" I groaned when her lips wrapped around my head again. Her mouth became a vacuum, sucking me down her throat. I grabbed a handful of her hair and pulled her away from me. I wasn't ready to come yet. The way she was topping me off, I would pass out when I came.

"Go to my bedroom and take that shit off," I said stroking my dick. She gave me a seductively smile, pulling her blouse over her head. Her nipples looked like they were going to bust through her lace bra. I followed behind her; she peeled clothes from her body as she walked down the hall. She climbed on the bed with her ass in the air; looking back at me, she made her ass cheeks jiggle and bounce.

I watched her spread her legs wide and play with her pussy. My mouth watered as she finger fucked herself. Pussy juice dripped down her hand as I walked over to her, gripping and spreading her ass cheeks. I licked and sucked her ass before fucking her ass with my tongue. My tongue slipped down to her pussy and twirled between her wet lips. She moaned and whimpered making my tongue turn into a cyclone.

"Fuck! Ooooohhhh! Chiiikkke!" She cried out baptizing me with her honey.

I flipped her over after drinking every drop from her. She lay shivering on the bed, as I climbed on top of her. She welcomed me inside her drenched hole, wrapping her legs around my waist. My dick slid slow and deep inside her, making sure to hit every sensitive spot she had. Crue arched her back when I sucked and bit on her hard nipples. My upper body laid on top of her with a curve in my back. Her walls strangled my dick every time she came. Tears slid down the sides of her face as her pussy cried a river.

"I can't stop," she whimpered softly as she exploded again. I could hear her wetness splashing from her.

"Keep coming on this dick," I groaned in her ear. I made love to her until my dick was ready to release its load. My strokes became harder, faster and deeper. Groans and grunts echoed through the room as I hammered inside her. She whispered in my ear.

"Come in my mouth."

I couldn't hold it any longer. I pulled out and stood on my knees. She quickly wrapped her hands around my shaft, jacking me with her hand and sucking me with her mouth.

"Aaaaarrrrggghhh! Gggggrrrrr! Ssssshhhhit!" My body jerked and twitched; my toes and abs locked up. I had never came so hard; the room felt like it was spinning. She was slurping and moaning as she drained me like she was sucking a milk shake through a coffee straw. I had to pull her head away, because she had my shit sensitive as fuck. She fell back on the bed giggling. I looked down at her.

"I'll fuckin' kill you, Crue," I said. The thought of her doing what she'd just done to me for another nigga made my blood boil. She laughed harder.

A Week Later

Jedrek

"**P**lease don't do this. She will live, but at what cost?" Vanity pleaded with me.

Last night, Zelda slipped into a coma after going into cardiac arrest, so today, regardless of how everyone else felt, I was going to save her life. Nothing Vanity said mattered. The only thing that mattered was saving Zelda. Before I let her die, I would risk her hating me. Echon wouldn't go against Zelda and Vanity to find a heart for Zelda, so I took matters into my own hands. Where the heart came from didn't matter to me, all I knew was it was going to save Zelda's life.

When I told Zelda about finding a donor, she was overjoyed. Her body was so weak, all she could do was give me a half smile with a tear running down the side of her face. She was so weak; she could barely form a complete sentence without getting short winded. I didn't care that I threatened my entire family, forbidding them from telling Zelda where the heart came from. Or that this was going to tear all of us apart. None of that mattered to me, only Zelda's life mattered. Everyone has their price, except Dr. Bailon; he wouldn't agree to perform the transplant. Today, Zelda was being transported to another hospital, because I had found a doctor that would accept the seven figures I was offering.

"This is wrong, Jedrek. This isn't what my baby would want, and you know it," Crystal said. Tony, Zelda's dad, remained quiet. Something told me, he was leaving the decision up to me.

"Transport is on the way up," a short, black nurse informed us, stepping in the room. Vanity cried softly and walked out the room, followed by Crystal. Tony stayed in Zelda's room with me.

Drekia has been my backbone through this all. She had been with Lil J while we rotated shifts at the hospital with Zelda. I waited for Tony to give me a lecture, but he never did. We sat quietly until transport walked into the room. I watched them closely as they moved Zelda from her hospital bed to the transport bed. After securing her fragile body onto the bed, we followed them to the elevator. We didn't want to wait for the elevator to come back up, so we took the stairs.

Vanity and Crystal stood in front of the hospital entrance watching them load Zelda on the transport van. I ordered them not to leave until valet returned with my car. After a few minutes, valet pulled up with my car. When I gave a hand gesture, the transport pulled off. Vanity, Crystal and Tony stood watching the transport ride away with Zelda. I put my foot on the gas to pull off but had to slam on the brakes. Crue and Dr. Bailon jumped in front of my car like two damn fools. I jumped out ready to body them. Dr. Bailon was breathing profusely, holding out his arm to keep me from knocking him out.

"We…have…a…heart," he said taking a deep breath between each word.

"What?" Everyone said in unison walking over to Dr. Bailon.

"She doesn't have time for that bureaucratic bullshit. That could take weeks," I told him. He may have a heart, but I was sure getting all the proper paperwork could take weeks.

"No, the…fa-mi-ly…," Dr. Bailon said trying to catch his breath before Crue interrupted him.

"Geez! For a doctor you sure are out of shape. It was four flights down the stairs," Crue said rolling her eyes at him.

"What's going on, Crue?" Vanity asked her.

"It's Special. Her family has given consent to give her heart to Zelda. They delivered her handsome baby boy by C-section two days ago. He's perfect. Everyone is saying their goodbyes to her right now," Crue said looking at me with tears in her eyes.

"We don't have time to see if she's a match," I told them turning and walking back to my car. I mourned for Chike, but right now I needed to be with Zelda.

"No, we don't have to wait. Dr. Bailon and Special's doctor have handled all the tests. She's a match, Jedrek," Crue told me. I looked from Crue to Dr. Bailon to see if they were absolutely sure. Neither of them blinked an eye.

"Call the transport back," I said before walking back into the hospital.

I stepped off the elevator to see Mrs. Clayton crying in her husband's arms. He made eye contact with me, but they weren't the malicious eyes that he gave me the day Special was shot. He simply nodded his head at me. I slowly walked to them, reaching my hand out to shake his. Whatever disagreement he may have with me or my lifestyle, I grieved for him and his wife. No parent should bury their child. He closed his eyes and shook my hand as he held his wife. He nodded toward Special's room. I slowly opened the door to see her lying there like a sleeping angel. She was an angel to Zelda. The machines were turned off, and Chike sat by her bed holding Krysta. Shyma stood beside them stroking Chike's back as he grieved for Special. Shyma took Krysta from Chike's arm.

"Let's give her another kiss goodbye," Shyma said. Sometimes having a child's mind is best. Krysta didn't fully understand the goodbye kiss she was giving her mother. They kissed Special on her cheek before walking out the room. Chike ran his hand over his face to wipe away his tears while he stood up. He reached out to shake my hand, but I pulled him in for a comforting, thankful, brotherly embrace.

"Thank you," I said. Some words would never describe a feeling.

"It wasn't me. It was Crue. It's the right thing to do," he said looking back at Special's peaceful, lifeless body. I walked over and kissed her on both cheeks.

"I do need you to do something for me," he said.

"Anything," I told him. I was indebted to him and Special's parents for life.

Four Days Later

Zelda's heart transplant was performed three days after Special was taking off life support, and I had cried and prayed every day for her and thanking God. Visitation was strict in the CTIC unit. Doctors and nurses were in and out of the room all day checking the many machines that beeped nonstop. To look at her, with the tubes connected to many parts of her body, you would think Zelda was dying. However, the heart monitor told a different story.

Her gift from Special sounded like a beautiful melody from a drum. I couldn't stay overnight, but I was there for the entire duration of visiting hours. She slept most of the time I was there. They kept her wrists in restraints to protect her from pulling at the tube in her mouth. Once again, she couldn't speak. But this time, she couldn't write. Many times, she would look at me with tears running down her face. I didn't want to reveal everything to her while her condition was still critical. My only answer was someone saved her life.

She gagged as the nurse removed the tube from her mouth. After the tube was removed, they released her wrists.

"I know your throat is sore and dry. It'll be that way for a few days, but ice chips will help. I'll get you some," the nurse said smiling at Zelda. When she walked out the room, Zelda turned her head to look at me. I smiled at her.

"You look like a werewolf," she said without cracking a smile. I laughed hysterically. My hair, mustache and beard hadn't been cut for over a month. My looks hadn't been a concern of mine.

"You sound like Scar," I told her jokingly. She tried to laugh but the pain wouldn't let her.

Six Months Later

Drekia

"Got damn, Drekia! Stop biting my finger," he said humping deep inside me. He was hitting me in the right spot and making me moan out loud.

"Stop covering my damn mouth then," I told him.

"Be-damn-quiet-and-I-will," he said ramming inside me between each word. I tightened my legs around his waist and began to wind my hips. His fingers dug into my ass cheeks.

"Yes baby, don't stop," I moaned softly in his ear.

"Fuck this pussy magic," he groaned. The coat closet was hot and dark, making us sweat as we brought each other to our final destination. My strapless baby doll dress clung to my sweaty body as his dick spread inside me. My nails clawed into his shit, digging into his back. He pulled the top of my dress down freeing my breasts.

"Aaaahhhh Quan," I whimpered as he licked and sucked my breasts. He grinded inside of me, pressing against my g-spot, and I exploded. I quickly covered my mouth when my scream almost erupted. My body shivered as tingles ran through me.

"Fuck!" Quan barked quietly. His body jerked as he unloaded inside the condom. He kissed and licked my neck until we came down from our high. I gave him a passionate kiss before releasing my legs from his waist.

"You got the moo juice," he said looking down at his cream covered dick. I giggled.

Quan started coming around, because Jedrek was teaching him the game. The more I saw the changes in him, the sexier he got. He caught me checking him out on several occasions, but when I made my move, he turned me down, knowing Jedrek would kill him for touching me. But like a man, he eventually gave in to his smaller head. When Jedrek found out, he blew a gasket, threatening to dismember Quan. His concern was that Quan would break my heart, but we were just having fun. Neither of us were looking for anything serious. He found out the baby wasn't his from whoever the female was, and I'd had years of hormones built up inside me that needed to be explored. Having sex was just like riding a bike. Once you've done it, you never forget.

"I'll go out first," I said. We were all at Jedrek and Zelda's house for a family cook out. I walked out of the closet fixing my dress. Crue stood down the hall with her hand on her hip, shaking her head.

"That's just nasty," she said smiling. I shot her my middle finger and stuck my tongue out at her. She laughed and walked away. I went to my old bedroom to clean up. I returned to the cookout by the pool to enjoy the family until it was time for me to slip away later.

*****

"Hi girl, come on in," Quaysha said with a big smile on her face. I passed her a bottle of wine. She went to the kitchen, popped the cork and poured us a glass. I watched her gulped down one glass and refill her glass.

"Girl, you should've come to the cook-out. We got lit," I said flopping down on her couch.

"I would've but I can't deal with looking at Crue. I don't know how y'all forgave her so easily for everything she did. She's the reason Zelda got shot, I got kidnapped and raped and Special died. If she hadn't brought her mess to Atlanta none of this would've happened. Chike is a weak ass nigga for falling for her," she said. I took the glass of wine she poured for me and sat it on the table.

"Yes, Crue brought her problems to Atlanta. You included," I said staring at her. Her eyes grew big.

"One thing I can say about Crue is she owned up to her mistakes. She learned and grew from the mess she brought with her. You didn't. I befriended you, hoping you would fess up to your part in all of this. But you are still playing the innocent victim role" I said.

"I admitted I helped her rob Khalil, but I was only trying to help my best friend," she said sadly.

I laughed. "Lil J's bedroom is next to Zelda and Jedrek's bedroom with an adjoining door. When you were there, the door was slightly opened. Just enough for me to hear the conversation. I heard you admit to faking your kidnapping and giving Khalil the code to Zelda's house. My ears also heard you admit to knowing Special was seeing Khalil. Like Zelda said, you sat there and let this all happen. The only reason you told Zelda was because you knew she was the only one that could save you from Jedrek."

She couldn't deny anything I said. Crocodile tears started to flow down her cheeks, but they weren't working with me. Some may disagree, but I blamed Quaysha for everything that happened. Had she not set up the fake kidnapping, none of this would've happened. Khalil would've either gotten his money from Crue, some kind of way, or been killed by Chike and Jedrek.

"I'm sorry. Please don't tell Jedrek and Chike. They will kill me," she said.

"Oh, I'm not going to tell them. It would be pointless to tell Jedrek, because Zelda wouldn't allow him to kill you. She's so grateful to have life, she forbids him from taking another life. Chike will kill you though. But I'd much rather watch you die for causing my family and friends so much grief. That wine you just chugged down is poisoned. In about two minutes, your entire body will become paralyzed and your heart will stop."

She immediately reached for her phone on the center table, but I grabbed it. She jumped up to get her phone from me but fell through the glass center table. She lay on the floor with her mouth and eyes wide open, unable to move. I sat and watched her struggle to breathe until she took her last breath, then I pulled out my phone.

"Thank you," I said.

"I'll make sure it's cleaned up," Yella Boy said on the other end of the phone. I stepped over Quay's body and walked out her apartment. No one would miss her. She was only relevant by association.

Epilogue

Prime's First Birthday

Zelda

My new heart was thriving, and my life was blessed. Everyone stood around the backyard singing Happy Birthday to my handsome, godsent son. Me and Jedrek adopted Special's son, Prime. I was shocked but overjoyed when Jedrek told me Chike wanted us to adopt Special's son. Her parents didn't want the responsibility of being full time parents, but they were more involved in his and Krysta's life with visitations every other weekend. They admitted they only kept her on the machine, because guilt was burdening them. Her parents felt if they hadn't turned their backs on her; she would still be alive today. It was never about wanting to be full-time parents to Special's baby. I was grateful to have them here at their grandson's first birthday. Finding out Special's heart was inside of me was overwhelming. I mourned for weeks over her death. It didn't seem fair that she had to die so young, but I was grateful for being given a chance to live a full life. I looked around the backyard at my family and friends, and all I could do was thank God for giving me another chance. Jedrek was out of the game and running his legit businesses while I was still enjoying being a housewife. I had decided to take another year off before returning to work. Jedrek slipped up behind me and wrapped his brawny arms around my waist.

Drekia sat talking with Vonna, Aunt Dee and Shyma. Their relationship had come a long way, but Vonna still loved her young men. Drekia was enjoying her womanhood with no boundaries. I smiled at my little cousin, Crue. She had become a young lady, and her and Chike's relationship had blossomed. He'd started growing his legit business building window frames Crue was still enrolled in school and had established a name for herself in Atlanta for her braids and locs. It made my heart flutter to see her playing and laughing with Krysta. My parents sat at a table conversing with the Claytons.

"Make sure you eat," Jedrek whispered, licking my earlobe. My pussy walls clenched. Sex between us was at an all-time high. We were fucking each other like barbaric animals and loving every minute of it. He walked away and joined Echon, Chike, Yella Boy and Quan at the card table. Yea, my family played cards at the kids' parties. Vanity walked over to me with a beautiful smile on her face and embraced me with a warm hug.

"Love wins all battles," she said hugging me tight.

"You can't fight love," I replied.

"Flying monkeys, unicorns, love and happiness," we said together.

THE END

For sneak peeks and future book releases follow Nona Day:

https://www.instagram.com/msnonaday/

https://www.facebook.com/nonadaynovels/

Nona Day's Romance Reading Group:

https://www.facebook.com/groups/137785320163038/

CPSIA information can be obtained
at www.ICGtesting.com
Printed in the USA
LVHW091622310719
626019LV00006B/978/P

9 781081 378844